MAGGIE: A GIRL AND NINE OTHER STORIES

KENNETH C. GARDNER, JR.

MAGGIE: A GIRL AND NINE OTHER STORIES

iUniverse books may be ordered through booksellers or by contacting:

iUniverse
1663 Liberty Drive
Bloomington, IN 47403
www.iuniverse.com
1-800-Authors (1-800-288-4677)

ISBN: 978-1-4917-9841-6 (sc)
ISBN: 978-1-4917-9842-3 (e)

Print information available on the last page.

iUniverse rev. date: 05/25/2016

Books by Kenneth C. Gardner, Jr.

Novels

The Song Is Ended (2011)
The Dark Between The Stars (2012)
Travels On The Road To America (2015)

Collections

Meatball Birds and Seven Other Stories (2013)
"And All Our Yesterdays…" and Nine Other Stories (2014)

Non-Fiction

Echoes of Distant School Bells: A History of the Drayton Public School, 1879-1998, Volume 1 (1994); Volume 2 (1999)

For my readers, both actual and potential:
I do not write "light and fluffy."

Contents

THE SNAPPER

W hat is the purpose of a snapping turtle?
In the *Song of Solomon* a turtle is mentioned as having a voice, but that turtle was a turtle dove, not the shelled reptile, so God didn't give humans any Biblical clues as to why the snapping turtle is here on earth.

Around the time of the Great War, Bear Cockburn (which, despite its spelling, is pronounced "Coh-burn") and his son Boss were fishing in the Great Northern reservoir just west of Menninger, North Dakota, when something took hold of Boss's hook, and just by the feel, Boss could tell it was something big.

He called to Bear to take his rod, kicked off his boots, and jumped in. The "res" had a shallow-water shelf that ran out from the shore and then tailed off into deeper water. Boss followed the line down and caught hold of a giant snapping turtle in six feet of water, trying to head off the shelf.

When Bear saw that Boss wasn't coming up, his boots went flying, and the sixty-eight year old man joined his son on the bottom. Working as a team—one up for air, one down fighting the turtle, then the other up and the first one down—they managed to bring the monster to shore.

They had to rest and recover before they could get the thing into the backseat of Bear's Cadillac. They built a pen for it in Boss's backyard, over the protestations of his wife.

They estimated that it weighed over fifty pounds, had a carapace-length of just over two feet, and looked pale green due to the little moss-like growth in the grooves of its shell. It was just a guess, but they thought it was possible that the snapper had been patrolling the Jacques River and later the res since the Lincoln-Douglas debates before the Civil War.

The pen they made had a big water hole in the middle, so the snapper could submerge, just the way it spent most of its life in the wild. The pen was a square of chicken wire wrapped around steel posts and stapled to old railroad ties at the bottom, so the reptile couldn't force its way under the wire in a break for freedom.

When people would come to view the largest turtle ever seen in central North Dakota, Boss would take a large rake and slide the animal up the muddy side of the water hole so everyone could "oooo" and "ahh" and sometimes little children would start to cry, it was so ugly. If it was in an especially bad mood, it would hiss so loudly that even some of the men would back away from the wire.

Children were always warned not to put their fingers inside the wire or they might get bitten off. Actually, that would never have happened unless the snapper was right next to the fence, and if that were the case, there were no children innocent enough to poke a finger through the wire.

After a couple weeks, the excitement of seeing a turtle that mostly looked like it was dead wore off and other things—the circus, the Independence Day parade and picnic, fireworks, dances, and other social events—cast it into the Land of the Forgotten. Even Boss's sons, Josh and Lige didn't bother with it.

So it was no surprise when it escaped.

It happened this way. A tremendous thunderstorm wracked the entire countryside one night, lightning and thunder scaring even the stoutest of men. The ground was saturated; roofs that had never leaked before, leaked; several cattle and horses were struck down in the pastures; people thanked the Lord for His Protection and for their indoor sanctuaries.

The snapper probably wasn't thanking anyone; it just got busy with its claws and dug its way through the saturated soil under the ties and wire and into freedom. Whether or not there is a homing instinct in snapping turtles or maybe just in ones that reached the age of almost sixty, the snapper started moving toward the west, toward the water from whence it had come. The snapper moved down the grassy strip just off the north side of Lamborn Avenue in a slow, but continual, jerky movement.

By false dawn the turtle moved onto the patchy lawn where the assistant printer of the *Menninger Messenger* lived and crawled under the drooping shelter of a spirea bush to wait out the day.

That night it crawled out to the strip of grass and began its laborious hitch-and-go crawl to the west, eventually reaching the lumberyard, where the grass ended. Crawling on the gravel and over stones was harder for the reptile, and it took quite awhile for it to reach the railroad tracks where it forced itself over the crossing. It still had a business block of buildings to travel and it was beginning to labor.

Just when it seemed all was lost, another storm broke, not as violent as the previous one, but with almost as much rain. The water rushed down the Lamborn hill, filling the shallow ditches alongside the street, and overwhelming the sewer system. The rush carried the snapper along with it, through the business section and on down Lamborn to where the hill smoothed out. The snapper found grass under its feet and clawed its way over to rest by an elm and recover from its wild ride.

Fred Oleson was a drunk and had been one since he discovered alcohol at the age of fourteen when he started nipping from a jug his older brother Eric kept in the barn.

When Eric and his wife Lena moved into town and built the Oleson House hotel, Fred tagged along and soon discovered Eric's jug in the hayloft of the hotel barn. When he volunteered for the Spanish-American War and ended up in Cuba, he discovered three things: he didn't like being shot at, Cuban girls, and Cuban rum.

After he left the Army, he vowed he'd never be a target again. He began to escort Kathleen O'Donnell around Menninger, and he started to visit the various blind pigs whose bootleg hooch satisfied the dependency his body had developed.

Being a drunk should disqualify a man from ever being a husband, but some women see it as a challenge and are determined that they can bring the man back to sobriety. Kathleen was such a woman. She'd seen her father drink himself to death, despite her mother's care and prayers, and she thought she could redeem Fred and, in that way, help make up for her father.

After they got married, Fred took over as the night clerk at the hotel, and Kathleen worked in the kitchen and as a maid. She was steady and reliable, but Fred was anything but. After a year he was demoted to housekeeping duties, and when he couldn't even be relied on to do that, he was told to take care of the barn, empty the spittoons, and help guests with their bags.

Fred realized to lose that job would pretty much end his drinking because neither Eric nor Kathleen would give him any money, so he mucked out the barn; cleaned out the tobacco juice, cigar butts, and spit; and carried luggage up one, two, or three flights of stairs, never complaining in hopes of a bigger tip.

Kathleen and Fred had a small cottage near the west end of Lamborn Avenue, which was a street that started at Winslow's pasture on the east side of Menninger and went gently downhill eight blocks to Fifth Street West, where the couple lived.

North Dakota had come into the Union as a "dry" state, but the blind pigs did their best to alleviate that problem for the thirsty. There were a couple "pigs" out in the country, but at least half a dozen flourished in town. The police officers realized that to forbid alcohol to a male population with large minorities of Scandinavians, Germans, and Irish was asking for trouble. Allowing those men to drink was trouble, too, but less so if they stayed indoors at the "pigs." No one wanted a bunch of boozy fellows singing and yelling and fighting on the streets in plain sight of ladies and children.

So it was that Fred had the funds and the sources for his habit. When he felt the urge, he'd stop in at a "pig" on Dakota, Villard, Chicago, or even the ones over on St. Paul and indulge until his coins and those of his friends were gone. Usually by that time, he was almost blind and had no sense of direction. No one was worried, however, because they'd point him at the railroad tracks and let him walk, or stagger, as the case may be.

Once he got to the tracks, he instinctively turned north and followed the rails to Lamborn, then headed west and gravity and inertia would eventually bring him home.

He hadn't done any drinking the night of the big thunderstorm, but he made up for it the next night. When he left the blind pig, he was pretty much blind himself, but managed to follow the tracks to Lamborn and take his familiar pattern toward home. However, when the rain came, he had to find shelter in the doorway of an empty building and wait it out.

When the rain moved on, he started down the hill, careening and lurching his way along. When he got to the flatter part, he suddenly passed out.

The snapper had seen a dark shape pass by its resting place, but within a few minutes took up its own journey. Its short legs thrust its heavy body westward at a steady pace. Soon the snapper became aware of something blocking its path, so it started around the thing.

Fred lay with his head on the grass and his body on the street. He came back from wherever his conscious mind had gone and opened his eyes. He saw an ugly head, a horrible beak, a greenish shell, long claws an inch from his face. He screamed. The Devil had come to take him! He screamed again, but his body was frozen; he couldn't get up. His next stop would be Hell!

Then the Devil opened its mouth and hissed.

Fred passed out.

When he came to, he was in his own bed. Kathleen was asleep in the chair beside him.

He never told her about meeting the Devil, but together they went to the next meeting of the WCTU, and he took the pledge never to use alcohol, a pledge he kept, to the surprise of everyone who knew him.

The snapper died later that fall, perhaps worn out by its arduous journey.

THE ABORTION

"Hey, Mac…I mean Mikey…see I got your name right. 'nother of the same for my friend and me. Put it on my tab and add a nice tip for yourself, but not over a fin."

"No, put your money away; it's no good here…Yuh know how I 'membered his name? 'cause it rhymes with Ikey, and that's right outta the past.

"Ikey wasn't his real name; it was Isaac. That's what his folks called him, 'cept Buddy called him Ikey. Buddy wasn't his real name, either; it was Lawrence. Yuh shoulda seen him when he was a senior in high school. There was a picture of a statue of David in one of our text books; o'course, it had a kind of leaf where his…his… well, you know. I guess in real life it shows. Anyway, Buddy looked like David, right down to his curly hair and slim build…we'd go swimmin' in the summertime.

"I fell for him when he was a senior and I was a sophomore. He sat a couple seats ahead of me in the Assembly Room, but off to the side, so I could see his profile. He had a straight nose, just like David. I'd write down "Mrs. Lawrence John McPhail" or "Mrs. Buddy McPhail" or "Mildred Mae McPhail" or "Millie McPhail" just to see which one I liked the best, but I liked 'em all.

"Later he told me he had noticed me the first time I walked into Assembly, but he didn't say or do anything, so it was a complete 'whamee' when he asked me to the Homecoming Dance.

"O'course, my father had to lay down all sorts of rules, and then, o'course, Buddy followed 'em to a 'T,' so the night wasn't all I thought it would be."

"Thank yuh, Mikey. Say, you're kinda young to be workin' in a place like this, ain't yuh?"

"Young! Yuh shoulda seen me on my first job. I had no intention of takin' it, but it was right after Buddy and I broke up, and I had to get away from Menninger, so I went to Fargo and worked in a little drugstore with a tiny lunch counter…This tastes better'n the first one…I guess I'm gettin' ahead of myself.

"After Homecoming…he was on the football team; he caught the ball…we started seein' a lot of each other, not goin' steady, but almost.

"When he asked me to the Winter Formal, my mother and I went all out. Had a new formal made by the milliner, better'n anything in the catalogues. My father took our pitcher, but it was black and white. Kept that pitcher for awhile after we broke up, but it's gone. Don't know where…or when…Water under the bridge, as they say.

"We'd go to the movies, sit in the back row of the Blackstone. I'd try to get him a little worked up, but no soap. He belonged to some church— Reformed German or German Reformed, somethin' like that. Mother was German, Kaufmann; his Dad was Irish Catholic, but converted. I was Congo…Congregational. Nothin' now. Haven't been inside a church since…

"There I go, off the rails again. Went to all his basketball games and baseball games. When he graduated, I sat with his family. They lived on a farm five miles outta town, so it wasn't easy for us. Besides, he had to help with the farm work; his Dad was sick. Buddy had an older sister; she helped out, too.

"First time I went to their farm was the first time I met Ikey. He was feebleminded, as they said back then. Today he'd be gifted in another way, or some such lingo. Fact was he couldn't talk, just grunt or point. He could walk around and even dress and feed himself, but he slopped the food down his chin and on his shirt so much I hated eatin' with him… He smiled a lot.

"Anyway, I was still in high school, but I had big plans for us after we got married. I'd get Buddy off the farm, and we'd go to the Twin Cities or Chicago, where I could get a job; it didn't matter what, just enough to pay a good teacher to help me perfect my piano playin' and singin'. I had talent; everyone said so. Buddy was a good mechanic; he knew everything about engines, so he could get a job anywhere.

"I had it all figured out by the time I graduated. I knew he loved me; he told me so. We hadn't done anything, he was so shy, but that wouldn't be a problem. I could tell he was red-blooded enough.

"Then the roof fell in. First, his Dad died. Then his mother. It was like she didn't want to live anymore, just kind of wasted away and gave up. Ever hear of anything so crazy?

"His sister—her name was…what was her name? Colleen? No, that wasn't it—well, it don't make no difference. His sister married a farmer's son and they took over the farm. Buddy stayed on and worked. That was all right. But he also started takin' care of Ikey.

"It was hardly ever Buddy and me; it was most likely to be Buddy, Ikey, and me. Sometimes Ikey would stay with the sister, and we'd go out, but not often enough for me.

"We'd never had a fight when I was in high school, but we started fightin' a lot because I said he thought more of Ikey than me, even though he denied it.

"I put my plans on hold for a year. I tried to be nice to Ikey, but no dice. I just couldn't warm up to that kid and his cockamamie smile.

"Farm prices had been good durin' the war, and they held up for a year or two after. One day Buddy called me; that was unusual, I almost always called him. He said he'd bought a car and wanted to take me to a fair in Minot. That would be some trip—about 120 miles. My parents were opposed, but Buddy said if we left early enough, he'd guaranteed we'd be home before dark. They liked Buddy so they let him convince 'em.

"When Buddy pulled into the yard in his 1917 Ford Model T Tourin' Car...see, I 'membered...I was in seventh heaven. You probably don't know what they were like—black, with spoked-wheels, runnin' boards, no bumper, big windshield, and front and back seats. Plus it was a convertible; the roof could be folded down and hang over the back a little.

"Then everything turned sour; Ikey was ridin' in the front seat."

"Hey, Mickey...Mikey...another over here. Did yuh see how I signaled him? I learned that in New York City, when I was in the big time...well, almost the big time. Oh, yeah. Yuh think you're just talkin' to some old broad, but I almost made it. My first husband Jake had connections with the Mob, and he got me into some of their clubs, but he got rubbed out, which was just as well 'cause he was pressurin' me to have kids. All those criminal types want a son to carry on after they're gone. Then I married Arnie, who took me all over the East Coast as part of the Wingate Trio. Yuh heard of 'em? Don't matter. Arnie's long dead and gone. He played the guitar and sang. I played the piano and did some singin'. Bernie...old Bernie...boy, could he play that doghouse bass! Gone, too; maybe they buried him in his bass. It was almost big enough. Well, true to form, Arnie wanted kids.

"Oh, I forgot to tell yuh. When I was married to Jake, my father died. When we showed up in Menninger, it didn't go over too well. Jake looked too much like what he was, and I was all dolled up in the latest fashions, drippin' with necklaces and jewels. My mother was not pleased. When Jake got gunned down, she refused to come East for the funeral. When she died, I was on the road with the Trio, so she was planted before I even knew she was dead.

"We had slack times when I was part of the Trio, couldn't get work. When that happened, Bernie would tend bar, I'd waitress, and Arnie would cook. He was a damn good cook, excuse my French. Well, we got this job at a resort in the Catskills; the handwritin' was on the wall for Prohibition, so the booze was out of the basement and back on the tables. Music and booze kind of go together, don't yuh think? Well, it don't matter. The country was in the toilet, but for those who could afford it, luxuries like a summer resort were cheap. The job would pay good, compared to what we'd been gettin', but it wasn't for two weeks, so I begged Arnie to take me to Menninger to visit the graves. He said we could go, if I'd have a baby. I told him I'd think about it. I did think about it for about ten seconds and came up with a big fat "No," but I didn't tell Arnie that.

"The graves were nice. My mother had provided in her will for a gravestone to match my father's. She'd gotten everything when my father died, and I got everything when she died, but it wasn't anywhere near what I expected. What did she spend her money...my money...on? Anyway, the Ladies' Auxiliary had done a nice job keepin' the cemetery up. We ate at a restaurant uptown and people kept comin' over and tellin' me how much they missed my mother and how much she'd done for 'em financially or for her donations to the various charity drives. Yeah, with my money. I could hardly wait to get outta there. But I had to do one more thing.

"I told Arnie I wanted to take a drive into the country, and I sort of directed him to the McPhail farm. They had gone bust and someone said they headed west, but he didn't know where for sure, maybe Oregon. Abandoned buildings on a farm seem to deteriorate faster than those in town. Paint was patchin' off, shingles were loose or gone, windows were broken out, the haymow door was hangin' by one hinge, corral busted down. I hadn't seen the place in almost twenty years, and everyone had cleared out maybe ten years before, but the whole thing looked like a hatchin' place for ghosts, weeds all over, swallows flyin' in and out of the chicken coop. I told Arnie to step on it. The ghosts could stay behind..."

"Where was I? I guess I kinda got off my story...Let's have one more drink and that'll be it. I can't have yuh thinkin' I'm a lush, and us just meetin' for the first time. Hey, there, Ikey! Oh, Jeez, did yuh hear what I called him? Uh...Mikey, the same over here."

"If yuh think drivin' to Minot was like it is today, think again. Just gettin' to Fishtown we were on country roads of gravel, and if the gravel got thin, hard packed dirt. I was ridin' like a sardine 'cause Ikey had to ride next to Buddy, so either I made friends with the door or sit in the back seat, which is where Ikey shoulda been. Actually, he shoulda stayed home. Buddy had a box in the back seat full of orange pop. He'd reach back there, grab a bottle, and give it to Ikey. I guess it was his favorite. Then came the strange part; I'd have to open it and put a nipple…yuh know, from a baby's bottle, on it, and Ikey would suck away.

"O'course, after we left Fishtown, Ikey had to go, so we had to stop where there was some bushes, and Buddy took Ikey behind 'em. Left me sittin' in the car on the road.

"At least we were on decent gravel by then, but what with the pop, Ikey was makin' us stop every half hour or so. I got so annoyed, I can't tell yuh. I'd never been up that way before, so I'd be askin' Buddy about the towns or the birds or the flowers we saw—Buddy knew a lot about such things—when Ikey would grunt, and Buddy would stop. When they got back to the car, I had to step out so Ikey could get in, and he'd smile at me. I couldn't tell if he was happy, or if he was smilin' 'cause he got to ride next to Buddy and I didn't."

"Here's the drinks. Thank yuh, Mikey. Did yuh add a tip like I told yuh? Good, add a little more…Ummm, that's smooth. Yours good, too?…Great."

"Well, outside of Dewey, it started to rain, so we had to put up the top. Lucky for us Buddy had brought some rain-proofs, so we spread 'em over us and kept goin'. Those cars were pretty much open—no windows—so the rain got in on the sides with no problem. Ikey liked the rain; I hated it.

"When we got to Minot, we drove right to the fairgrounds and got somethin' to eat. I wasn't used to goin' so long without eatin' and made a pig of myself. We checked out the animal barns because Ikey liked the horses, cows, pigs, sheep, and especially the chickens. I couldn't stand the smell, especially where the chickens were kept, and I almost threw up. Buddy held onto Ikey's hand and said the names of all the animals, as if Ikey would ever remember.

"They had some smaller rides for kids and Ikey rode on 'em. Buddy and I never got to ride because Ikey was too scared to go on any of the bigger rides, even the Ferris Wheel. We ate some more, and Buddy bought Ikey some cotton candy, so his hands and face got sticky.

"Buddy had been to Minot several times, so I asked him to show me the town. For all we didn't get to do at the fair, I figured he owed me that. We drove around downtown, but Fargo was bigger and better. Finally, Buddy said he'd take me up North Hill.

"It was a gravel climb and after we got up, it wasn't a knobby hill like you see in a picture. Everything was flat; it was only a hill because we had been down in the Mouse River Valley. Buddy turned off onto a road and then turned again toward the city on a little trail that was wet from the rain. We could see the buildings going up South Hill, but Buddy said he wanted to show me the river and the railroads and kept goin'.

"Suddenly we could see where the hill ended. Apparently, some construction company had excavated part of the hill and created a sheer drop-off. Buddy cranked the wheel, and the car turned sharp, but the door sprang open, and I went sailin' out. I wasn't hurt, but I was on a muddy slope that led directly to the cliff, and I was movin' fast. There was a bush growin' on the lip, and that was what saved me. I crashed into it and hung on for dear life. A few seconds later a big weight smashed into me.

"It was Ikey, and he kept slippin' on the mud and began goin' around me. His legs were over the edge when I grabbed his hand and stopped him. I worked my body around the bush and got my other hand on his arm. I looked uphill and the Model T was on its side, and Buddy was tryin' to work his way to us, but whenever he tried, he started to slip and had to crawl back.

"Now that I think about it, he looked just like my third husband Harold when he was so drunk he couldn't stand up. O'course, that was a long time after Arnie. When the lid came off Prohibition, we really got the jobs, playin' the new clubs and hotels. People might not have a lot of money, but they had money for good booze after the swill they'd been payin' for when the country was 'dry.' 'Dry?' That's a laugh.

"And then we began gearin' up for war with the draft. The boys wanted their booze and some live music, so the Wingate Trio was in demand. Pearl Harbor, and you're twenty or twenty-one and far away from home. Some liquor, some music, they sooth the pain.

"That was when we were within a cat's whisker of makin' it. We auditioned for our own radio program. Yeah, it was gonna be on Mutual, the poor man's network, but it was national radio. Only they chose to go with a singer instead. It really broke Arnie's heart. Oh, we kept playin', but singers like Frank Sinatra, Perry Como, Vaughn Monroe, Dinah Shore, Jo Stafford, were comin' in, and we were slowly goin' out. Arnie kept askin' if we could have a kid. I told him I was over forty, so 'No.' He died of a heart attack right after our last show in Buffalo, New York, a helluva place to die in. It shoulda been New York City.

"I was single for a couple years and shoulda stayed that way. I met Harold after I'd gone solo and worked the supper clubs. He was no good, but I needed someone, or thought I needed someone, but I didn't need someone who would drink up everything I made while he sat around and did nothin' but drink up everything I made. Finally, I got a divorce in Reno and started workin' the West Coast—California and Oregon— for a change…Didn't find what I was lookin' for, so here I am in Vegas, playin' the little places when I was almost big.

"Oh, yeah, I got off my story again…Ummm. Good to the last drop doesn't just apply to coffee, huh?...Anyway, Buddy yelled down to me, askin' if I could hold on. That bush wasn't goin' anywhere, and I had a good grip on Ikey's hand and coat, so I yelled up that I did. I was young and strong; when my mother needed a jar opened, she'd ask me. Buddy yelled he was goin' for help and took off runnin'.

"So there I was, left alone, where I didn't want to be, and holdin' on to what? I looked down and Ikey gave me that stupid smile. When you thought about it, he wasn't really human. A collie dog could do just about everything he did, and when a collie got old, you put it down without a second thought.

"He was gettin' heavier. He couldn't help by pullin' his legs up over the lip. Even if I asked him, he wouldn't understand. Then I got to thinkin'. What kind of life would Buddy and I share with Ikey hangin' around? He would always drag us down. Maybe Buddy would never leave the farm, and my career would be kaput before it even got started.

"I looked at Ikey close. I swear I could see orange around his mouth and pink cotton candy on his fingers; he had mud on his face, his hands, his clothes, and in his hair; he was a mess; he'd always be a mess. He'd be Buddy's mess; he'd be my mess. Then he grunted and I knew what that meant.

"I told him not to, to hold it…and then he wet his pants. I watched the liquid run down and over the edge…and I let go.

"He didn't make a sound.

"I didn't feel anything; nothin' bad, nothin' good. I just held onto the bush, and I think I may have dozed off because the next thing I knew Buddy was up the hill yellin', askin' where Ikey was. Not how I was.

"He and some other men lowered a rope with a loop in it and pulled me to safety. Buddy grabbed my shoulders and asked where Ikey was. I pointed down the hill and said I couldn't hold on any longer.

"Other men had brought ropes, so he had 'em tied together, got in the loop, and had 'em lower him over the edge. Pretty soon we heard Buddy yell to pull and slowly Ikey came up through the mud. The men stayed back on the grass to pull; none of 'em wanted to slide over the edge.

"Someone put a jacket over Ikey's face. He lay in the grass like a mud-covered bag of clothes with feet. The men had to tie on a small log to get the rope down to Buddy. When they got him up, he didn't say a word to me, just went over and hugged Ikey and cried and cried.

"I'll spare you the details of reportin' the accident and gettin' the body back home. I didn't wanna go to the funeral because I knew it was all over between Buddy and me, but I went. I didn't sit with the family.

"Buddy was still cryin'; I didn't know anyone could have that many tears.

"A few days later I called him up to tell him I was leavin' for Fargo. I was hopin' he'd at least come to the station to see me off, but he didn't.

"So that's my sad tale. Guess you've heard plenty of 'em…Your room or mine?…O.K. by me…Say, what's your name again?"

THE HA'NT AND THE
WOMAN IN WHITE

———————— ✺ ————————

"Young boys love to play pranks; they surely do. I was no different." My grandfather Boss was eased into the sofa and telling me the ways things were. I was eight and grounded for putting an ant down Mary Richie's back. She was nine and lived across the alley. I liked her and it was supposed to be a joke, but it was a piss ant and bit her. She went home crying, her mother called my mother, and retribution was not far behind.

When I was grounded, no one was allowed to talk to me. I had to sit and be quiet until suppertime. But Boss was different: Mom didn't try to stop him when he walked slowly into the room.

"Well, well, what have we here?"

I told him and tried to keep from crying—not because I had any remorse, not because I had lost almost an entire afternoon of fun, but because I was embarrassed. I never wanted Boss to think less of me.

He spoke quietly so Mom couldn't hear and said I was surely a chip off the old block—my Dad had not been a Little Lord Fauntleroy when he was young—and he launched into stories he had told me several times, but I still enjoyed hearing them, about how Dad and two of his friends had blown up a new sewer project in the west end of town with a large firecracker one Fourth of July when he was sixteen, and about how Dad and his two friends were up in the courthouse dome, trying to bat pigeons with a broom when Dad slipped and his foot went right through the ceiling of the court room just below while court was in session, and the defense attorney started yelling for a mistrial.

When Boss left, I put my arms around him and he hugged me. I had been close to some of my friends' grandfathers: a couple smelled like alcohol, some of them reeked of tobacco, and Tim Curtis from the west side of town had a grandfather who carried the odor of gasoline because he was always tinkering with an old car that was basically falling apart.

Boss never drank or smoked and let mechanics work on his Buick. He smelled like the first breath of air you take when you go outside after a rain—clean and crisp with nothing distracting from the moment.

Mom wasn't one to deny any of her children supper for their misdeeds, so I ate with the family, but right afterward it was back to solitary—no radio, no comic books, no toys. My teenage sisters Barbara and Marjorie were not allowed to talk to me, so after they had finished the dishes and walked into the living room, Dad took me up to my room for an early bedtime.

After I had gotten undressed, brushed my teeth, and said my prayers, he tucked me in and then sat on the bed. I couldn't help it; I started to cry.

"You know, Chris, what you did was wrong. You hurt someone."

"But I didn't mean to."

"That's good, but the point is you did. When you see Mary again, you can apologize, but that's just words. If you're really sorry, you can show it, not just say it. Choose her to be on your team or share something with her, maybe talk to her more."

"I am sorry. I...I wish I hadn't found that ant."

We were quiet for awhile and my tears dried up, then he said, "Pranks can be fun, but not if someone gets hurt...or maybe if you have a sympathetic policeman."

"What's that mean?"

"I guess I'll tell you about some of my pranks and maybe then you'll see. When I was growing up all the land a block east of us and up the hill was Winslow's pasture. Fourth Street wasn't much of a street, just a two-wheeled path through the grass. I was a few years older than you are now and thought it was a perfect place for an ambush.

"I rigged up a dummy in old clothes and a slouch hat and faked-up a face with some paint on a bag. I sneaked out to the pasture in the dark and rigged up the dummy so it was mostly upright, but hidden by the grass and weeds. I tied a rope around it, hid in the ditch on the opposite side, and waited.

"A couple farmers came by in their wagons and then Mrs. Ankrim in her Baker Electric. It didn't make much noise and was already past me before I could react. Then nothing. I was about ready to go home when Moses Wylie came along. He didn't like kids. We called him 'Old Man Mose.'

"He was in his Wolfe Touring Car and that made a lot of noise. He'd gone by train to Minneapolis and bought the car at the H.E. Wilcox Company, then he drove it all the way to Menninger. It had almost a foot and a half of clearance, and he probably needed all of it because the roads were not very good.

"Anyway, when he was chugging along, trying to avoid the ditches, I pulled on the rope, and the dummy flashed out of the high grass into his path. He didn't have time to react and ran right over it. I could see the car lift and go down twice, then I took off and hid behind the barn on the alley. They use it as a garage today.

"At first Wylie was remorseful, saying, 'I'm sorry! I'm sorry!'

"Then he climbed down, went around to the back, and kneeled down. When he discovered the dummy was just that and not a man, he started yelling and cursing. I won't repeat what he said—someday you'll hear all the words. When he got back in the Wolfe, he yelled, 'I got your rope!'

"I didn't care; it was an old one. It was worth it to get back at Wylie and all the times he would yell at us when we walked by his place on the public sidewalk, not even on his grass."

Sometimes when I went to bed, Dad would tell me a story. Maybe about a boy my age in a wagon train going West or a boy my age hunting or fishing and making a spectacular shot or landing a gigantic fish, but the dummy story was better because it was true. I snuggled over closer to him. "Tell me another one."

"Well, let's see. Once I played a ha'nt."

"What's that?"

"It's what people in town called me; it's a…like a ghost or a banshee, something unknown and scary. A year after my dummy trick I was fiddling around with a rope when I saw an old wood shingle. When I held it up, it looked like the wing of an airplane, and I got to wondering if it would act like one, so I bored a hole in one end, put the rope through it, and knotted it. Then I whipped it around my head, lariat-style. It acted somewhat like a wing, but what really got my attention was the sound— kind of an eerie whirring. I wondered what I could do with it.

"Sometimes things just pop into my head. I remembered a swampy place down east of the Great Northern depot, a perfect hideout. Before the GN right-of-way was built up, it was like a small creek, especially in the spring, but the railroad had cut down its size. You've seen it."

"Yeah, it's by the turkey plant."

"And even smaller now. Anyway, I hid my rope and shingle in the willows and waited for Saturday night. Back then just about every farm family and a lot of those in town did their shopping on Saturdays, and many of them stayed late.

"First chance I got, I headed for the swamp. The center of town was crowded and I had to wait for the band to stop playing. When it did, I began whirling the rope and shingle, and the weird noise headed up the hill toward downtown.

"I didn't do it steadily, and in the breaks I'd crawl out and see what was happening. At first, nothing, but then I saw some men come down Chicago Street to Dunnell, looking toward the GN. I ducked back into my hiding place and really gave the rope a good twirling. When I looked, the men had started walking down Chicago where it slopes, and I could see them gesturing and even hear some indistinct words.

"I had my plan. I scooted west through the willows, pulled the rope out of the shingle, threw them on a pile of railroad trash, and ducked low until I got to Dakota. I went up the hill to Dunnell and walked it east to Chicago, joining up with a lot of other boys, men, and even some girls and women. No one could figure out the noise. They ruled out a train and any known animals, such as cows, horses, or pigs, that might be in the stockyards, or dogs and cats that might be in the swamp.

"When someone mentioned a ghost, I felt good, but when a man from Missouri who worked on a local farm in the summer and fall said he thought it might be a 'ha'nt,' I felt great.

"Walking home, I knew my trick was better than I thought it would be. Even Boss and Ma, who had been uptown, were mystified.

"The next Saturday was even better; more people edging their way into the swamp, a lot more talk of ha'nts, and even expressions of fear from some of the girls and a few women, which caused some of the men to tell them they had nothing to fear: they'd stop whatever it was.

"It rained the next Saturday, but the next weekend was dry. It was my best night yet, with people coming down from Divide and up from Caseyville to try and capture the ha'nt. After I whirled the shingle more than I ever had and circled around up Dakota and over, there must have been two hundred people rushing down the hill. Many of the men and boys were swearing they would capture the ha'nt, including your Uncle Josh. When I heard all those vows and promises, especially from my older brother, I made plans for an even better night, but that didn't work out.

"At supper the next Friday, Boss said that there would be a surprise for the ha'nt Saturday night. There would be men hidden near the depot, in the trees south of the GN, and on the far side of the Northern Pacific right-of-way which was half a block to the east of the swamp.

"My heart fell when I heard that: it wasn't fair. But I also recognized the danger. Sometimes you can bait a trap for a weasel, get rid of all your scent, and think everything is just right, but if that big stoat is at all suspicious, he'll hightail it away despite that succulent fresh meat bait and all your plans.

"I 'hightailed' it, let the 'Ha'nt of the Swamp' die, and lived to prank another day."

"Did Boss know it was you?"

"You know, I never did ask him…Are you ready to sleep?"

"Tell me one more."

"All right, but then it's sleep for you."

"O.K."

"A year later we were in the War, so there was some talk about German spies, even though all the Germans around Menninger were good Americans. Still, people were on edge. Then a woman escaped from the insane asylum in Kingston. She had knocked out a nurse and walked out in her white uniform.

"Later that night some men saw her in the rail yards, but she told them she didn't need any help; she was just taking a short cut home. They actually thought she was a nurse and didn't think much of it until they heard the news of the escape.

"She must have gotten on one of the trains headed up the branch line because when the train went through Needham, the station agent saw a woman in white in the doorway of a boxcar.

"The next time she was seen was when she walked into the dining room of the Pierce Hotel in Caseyville. You've seen it—the big brick hotel facing the railroad tracks."

"Oh, yeah, we ate Sunday dinner there once."

"That's right. Well, it's the same building, but back then it was a lot nicer; people called it a showcase. Anyway, she ordered a big meal and when the waiter brought the bill, she asked where the Ladies' Room was. He pointed down a hallway, and when she headed in that direction, he went about his business. The lady went through the kitchen and out a back door; the cooks were the last people to see her.

"When her story was reported in the newspapers, it turned out she had attacked her husband with a hat pin."

"What's that?"

"Women used to wear large hats and to make certain they stayed in place, they would put a long pin through the hat and their hair, and it would keep the hat on their head. Some of them could even be this long." (He held his hands apart maybe ten inches.)

"Wow, that would hurt."

"Yes, it would, so people were afraid of her. And that made it perfect for me. Ma had stored some clothes in an upstairs closet, so I found an old white dress. I also took a white cloth flour bag from the back of the pantry, cut it, folded it into a triangle, and made a white scarf. I wanted a white hat with a long hat pin because that would give everyone that saw me a chill, but Ma didn't own a white hat and, anyway, I wasn't going to let anyone get near enough to see any pin.

"The *Menninger Messenger* had come out on Thursday, warning people to beware of the 'Woman in White,' that she was dangerous, and that she might be anywhere along the branch line.

"After Boss, Ma, and Josh left for downtown on Saturday night, I got ready. I told them I might be down later, but I knew they wouldn't miss me: Boss and Ma would talk to their friends, and Josh would find some of his high school pals and maybe even some girls to talk to.

"I hustled over to the north side of the court house, got into the shadows, and dressed up in white, making certain the scarf hid most of my face. Then I walked down the alley to Glen Haven and turned left to Villard. I could see a large crowd two blocks west on Chicago, so, after I checked to see that no one was coming down Villard from the east, I stepped into the street and slowly walked across.

"I was disappointed: no one saw me. I moved to the middle of the block and walked across Villard again. That time I got results: a woman screamed. Then I heard a male voice: 'It's the Woman in White!'

"That caused a big hullabaloo—woman and girls screamed; men and boys yelled; I felt great. Then some men, boys, and even some girls came charging up Villard. I took off for the back of the courthouse, where I had stashed a long black buggy cloak that Boss had, wrapped it around my shoulders, and headed for home."

"Why did you wear the cloak?"

"White shows up too well, even on a dark night. The moon wasn't anywhere near full, but there was enough light to give me away, so I wore black."

"Gee, Dad, you're smart."

"Well, I don't know about that. Anyway, when I got home, I raced upstairs and listened at my bedroom window to all the people going by. I thought it was glorious fun—all that uproar, threats, pledges, and promises of revenge on the Woman in White when they caught her.

"When I thought it was safe, I walked downtown and joined Boss and Ma, who told me all about the big event I had missed. Then Ma said

I couldn't be out alone anymore until the Woman in White was caught. I really had to get my brain churning because I didn't want my fun to end.

"Then on Thursday the *Messenger* came out with a front-page story on the Woman in White. It even said some officials from the asylum had come up to investigate. I could hardly stop from telling Boss I was the Woman.

"The next Saturday I laid off...didn't want to ruin a good thing, and the next Saturday I got lucky because Boss and Ma were going out to a social at the Buckingham Township Hall and wouldn't be home until late. Ma told me to stay in the house, but she let Josh go out, which I didn't think was fair.

"I got ready behind the court house, but that night I turned north on Glen Haven, turned west at the Catholic Church, and walked down Lamborn almost to St. Paul before a cry went up and the chase was on.

"I threw on the cloak and ran up the south side of the alley, past the sheriff's house and the Baptist Church to the school yard, always trying to run in the shadows of the trees, bushes, and the one stable on that side. I went around the school and dropped into a basement window well. I threw the cloak over me and lay down. I figured that no one would have a flashlight, and if anyone looked down the well, all they would see was black.

"Sure enough, some people did come over to the well—I could hear them; in fact, two of the voices were Merle and Pearl Potman, my two best friends—but either no one looked down the well or if they did, they didn't see anything.

"My heart was beating so fast, I thought someone would hear it and got ready to make a break for it, but then the last of the voices went away. I waited for a long time before I climbed out and walked home. When Boss and Ma heard the Woman had been spotted again, Ma asked me if I had stayed home. All I said was that I was safe, which was true enough.

"The next Saturday I didn't go downtown with Boss and Ma: I thought it might be suspicious if I went with them and the Woman never appeared. I stayed home and read some in *Treasure Island* and *Tom Sawyer*.

"Merle and Pearl told me a bunch of men were going to lay for the Woman the coming Saturday. Some of them would be on Villard near the courthouse and some of them would hide on Lamborn near the Catholic Church. When they asked me if I was going to be out, I told them Ma said I had to stay in.

"I had some thinking to do. I needed a good plan because there would be men on both sides of my escape route. I finally decided I had to have help so I went to Merle and Pearl.

"When I told them I was the Woman in White, they didn't believe me, so I had to show them my disguise. That filled them with admiration and probably some jealousy. When I told them my plan, they were enthusiastic and said they couldn't wait.

"On Villard there was a small building; no one could ever make a go of whatever they tried there—confectionary, meat market, ice cream parlor—so it was sitting there abandoned again. It's still there; you can see the word 'Confectionary' near the top in faded paint."

"Yeah, I've seen it."

"The twins and I had found a way to jimmy open the back door and then lock it from the inside; we thought of it as a sort of clubhouse. Anyway, I dug up a second costume for Merle and we put it in the building, and on Saturday night we met in the Potmans' backyard, coordinated our plans, and headed downtown. I couldn't let Boss or Ma or Josh see me, so I kept going up Stimson while the twins made their way through the big crowd on Chicago and then to the building via an alley. I went down St. Paul to the lumberyard where I had stashed my disguise and got dressed, then I crept along the side of the creamery to Lamborn and watched the mob.

"When there was a shout from those near Villard, and I saw people running east, I knew Merle had gone into action. After he had dressed in white, he was to sashay onto Villard and as soon as people saw him, he was to run between the brick lawyer's office and the small building, get inside, and lock the door. When the men came searching, Pearl would be in the alley and yell that the Woman went south toward the railroad tracks.

"It was a great plan—I saw men emerging from hiding places along Lamborn and head south, and I could hear the shouting of those on Villard. I went to the back of the creamery and waited. After a half hour or so, I walked back to Lamborn and looked down to Chicago; the men, or at least most of them, had returned. If some of them had gone back to their hiding places on Lamborn, I'd be caught, but I had to chance it. I stepped into the streetlight on the corner.

"Immediately, a woman screamed, 'There she is! The Woman in White!' I took off running up Lamborn, went left at the corner of the lumberyard and up a north-south alley which branched to the east. I took the branch, picking up my cloak which I had hidden there. A block-and-a-half and I'd be home.

"As I ran, I could hear the noise of the crowd in the distance which was normal, but what wasn't normal was the crunching of gravel a half block or so behind me. At first I thought the big hound that belonged to the press operator at the *Messenger* had gotten loose and was running after me. I'd see him tied up when I walked the alley; he was always friendly and wagging his tail, so I wasn't scared, but whatever was hitting the gravel behind me made a lot more noise than a dog would have.

"When I crossed Salem, I knew I was losing ground. I couldn't run into our house; whoever it was would see me. For sure I couldn't outrun the chaser even if I hadn't been forced to hold up my dress. I had to hide, but where?

"Larson's barn loomed up. I sprinted around to the south side, opened the door, and ran in. And tripped on my dress. And fell."

I began to laugh. "You wore a dress; that's funny."

"Yes, I guess it is, especially as I look back. Anyway, when I fell, I hit my head on one of the big rocks that was part of the foundation."

"Daddy, were you hurt?" I was concerned.

"Well, I got knocked out. When I came to, a light was shining in my eyes. I covered my eyes and sat up.

"A voice said, 'I thought it was you, Lige.' He pointed his light down and I saw his face. It was Jimmie Pike, one of Josh's high school friends and the fastest guy on the Muskrats' track team.

"I put my back against the wood of a stall and sat with my head in my hands. I said, 'What're you doing chasing me? I didn't do anything bad.'

"He laughed and said, 'Don't tell the old ladies around town; you scared 'em half to death.' I didn't say anything, so he said, 'After the mayor hired me as a special deputy (he pulled open his coat and there was a badge pinned to his shirt), Josh and I couldn't figure out why the Woman in White would be stupid enough to hang around Menninger week after week with half the country looking for her; even if she's crazy, she'd see she should keep movin'. After figurin' the Woman really wasn't the Woman in White, we tried to guess who it could be and by a process of elimination we came to you, especially since the Woman had disappeared so close to your house. When you took off down the alley toward your house, I knew it was you; even if yuh had gotten away from me, Josh is waitin' for yuh at your back door.'

"I knew I was defeated. All I could say was 'Now what?' and expect the worst: jail or being turned over to Boss and Ma.

"I was relieved to hear Jimmie say, 'Now nothin', I guess; you're not dumb enough to dress up again, are yuh?'

"I breathed a relieved 'No.'

"He pointed and said, 'Then get in your house. Everyone else went by up the alley fifteen minutes ago.' I had gotten up and opened the door when he said, 'Lige?'

"I turned. 'Yeah?'

"Jimmie's voice sounded envious: 'Josh and I wish we had thought of it.'

"I felt really good as I walked up to our back door."

"Dad, did Boss and Grandma ever find out?"

"They never said anything, but if Jimmie and Josh figured it out, I'm sure they had a pretty good idea, too."

"Boss and Grandma must have let you stay out late, huh?"

"Yes, I guess they did. They trusted me not to get into too much trouble."

"Dad, when can I start staying out late?"

He looked at me with just the hint of a little smile. "In a few more years, Chris, when you're old enough and as long as you don't get into trouble."

"I won't, Dad."

"Now it's way past time for you to be asleep." He snugged the blanket around me and stood up. "I love you, son. Good night."

"I love you, Dad."

Long after he had closed the door, I lay in my bed plotting some pranks when I got old enough.

THE UNMENTIONABLE

Officially, the United States has no aristocrats; unofficially, there have been plenty around.

A characteristic of the aristocrats is never to display emotion in public. Most of the time that rule is adhered to. That doesn't mean they don't have to face problems and bad situations which can gouge them pretty deeply; it's just they can't display their feelings to the rest of us.

In Colonial times there were the Southern planters—families such as the Byrds, the Carters, the Randolphs, the Lees, the Carrolls.

After the Revolution the northern states were too busy with democracy to have an aristocracy. Not so in the South: slave owners had complete control over the lives of their slaves and thus showed themselves to be authentic aristocrats. As the years rolled on, the slave owners became even more righteous in their defense of aristocracy to the point of designating some people as "white trash," and believing that bloodlines, social status, and dedication to a "Cause" would overcome the products of industry—massive employment of guns, ammunition, and railroads, which poured out of the factories of the North.

The Civil War ended the Reign of the Southern Aristocrats, but not of American aristocracy. While the South foundered in its own folly, Northern society then became dominated by the "Captains of Industry," the New York 400, and their families—the Rockefellers, the Astors, the Vanderbilts, the Depews, the Winthrops, the Roosevelts, the De Peysters, the Morgans, the Mellons, and various and sundry others, many of whom actually benefitted the vast bulk of Americans economically, albeit not as much or as fast as their critics demanded.

Then came the turn of the century and the advent of the "flickers." Soon we had the Aristocracy of Adulation: the movie stars and later the radio stars. For a change those aristocrats were actually loved by the common people, at least in a superficial way.

In Stevens County, Dakota Territory (subsequently, North Dakota), there was an aristocracy, too. It began even before there was a county, but the land had been surveyed by the government.

In upstate New York a young couple got married—Edward Blackwell and Charlotte Scarborough.

The Blackwells didn't come over on the *Mayflower*, but they weren't too far behind. They lived in Massachusetts for awhile, then moved to New York.

The Scarboroughs immigrated to Virginia to flee the Unmentionable that had happened in England, but a branch of the family moved north. The same Unmentionable had happened in Virginia—no one outside the family was quite certain what, but whatever it was, it was left behind in Virginia as the Scarboroughs escaped to New York.

Primogeniture was an Old World custom in which the first-born legitimate son inherited all the property belonging to the family. In addition, fee tail insured that the inheritance would remain within the family from generation to generation. While primogeniture and fee tail gradually lost influence in America, they remained a presence in some colonies and later a few states into the nineteenth century.

Edward Blackwell was the second son and primogeniture left him out in the cold. There were other young men like him, shut out of their old life and looking for a new one, profitable if possible.

Dakota Territory held out a promise of hard work, but also an opportunity to build a landed estate to replace the one in which Edward had been denied even part-ownership. He decided to move west. He spoke with other young men and sometimes their wives; together they organized an expedition to claim new land and start a new life.

Edward's older brother Daniel was agreeable to the plan. After all, it would put half a continent between the brothers and eliminate any friction caused by Edward's remaining on the estate. Daniel agreed to help finance the venture and even help Edward once he got started in Dakota.

Edward told his friends he was going because he had "land hunger" and wanted to see his crops growing on his own land.

Charlotte was enthusiastic. She told her family she wanted to go to Dakota Territory to help provide people with a better life.

Charlotte's two sisters were in their mid-twenties—Old Maids—and had chosen that way of life, haunted by the Unmentionable that afflicted the Scarborough family and determined not to allow it to surface again. They adamantly opposed Charlotte's marriage, but the wedding took place anyway, and the Blackwells left for Dakota Territory with a small group of homesteaders.

They rode the trains south of the Great Lakes to Chicago, passed through the Twin Cities, and ended up in Grand Forks, where they hired wagons and went land-looking. The Red River Valley was already filled with homesteads, plus the land had suffered a major flood earlier that spring which caused the settlers to reject any idea of living on such a flood-prone plain, so they drove west and climbed out of the Valley.

The little wagon train started crossing the drift prairies and working up and down coulees and around sloughs. Freed from the constant tamp of buffalo herds, the spring land was alive with the pink and green of prairie rose bushes. Far ahead a figure was seen walking toward them, and soon a Dutchman emerged from the flatness and told them he was heading for Grand Forks for supplies. They asked him where his horse was, and he said he didn't own one. When they told him they were homesteaders, he explained where he had his claim and that there was a fine flat-bottomed valley a few miles west of it that would hold them all. The wagons swung off to the southwest.

They entered the Ft. Sully Indian Reservation without knowing it, saw the large poplar grove to the northwest and a range of hills to the west, and forded the Divide River. Some of the men wanted to turn back: the rocky hills were not farmable, the land couldn't be fertile because there were few trees, and what kind of settlers would try to homestead without a horse—only the crazy kind like that Dutchman—but Blackwell kept them on their course, the horses fighting the marshy sloughs, straining up the elevations, and sliding down the ravines.

The hill known as Two-Humps bulged out of the earth to the south and a large lake mirrored blue to the west. Waterfowl rippled the water and red-wings scolded from the reeds.

They worked around the lake and kept heading into the sun. A few more sloughs and hills and then into the valley, where they camped. To the west they could see the "Hill."

The "Hill" was actually a rise of ground level with the land to the south of it, but it overlooked the lower land to the east, north, and west which had been smoothed out by water from the melting glaciers while the "Hill" was untouched.

The Blackwells had first choice of land, so they claimed 160 acres, some on the northeast side of the "Hill," where they put up a claim shack over the next few weeks, and the rest down in the valley. They also claimed an additional 160 acres under the Timber Culture Act. The other settlers claimed land in the valley, and a post office was established with the grand name of Buckingham. That winter most of them went back to New York to get more of their property and to induce others to come west.

The next spring several dozen settlers took the Northern Pacific into Kingston and carted their belongings north on the old Ft. Sully Trail. They occupied most of the valley and some even became hill farmers to the north and east.

That fall smoke on the western horizon marked the work locomotives as the branch line of the Northern Pacific was pushed north of Caseyville and marked the birth of the new town of Menninger.

The Blackwells knew a challenge when they saw one and helped set up a general store on the "Hill" just west of their claim. A blacksmith set up shop a little while later and soon there was a township hall. But when harvest came, the wheat had to be transported to the railroad at Menninger, so the Blackwells began casting around for a railroad to build into Buckingham. There were a few nibbles, but no bites.

Fewer people went back to New York the second winter and more came out in the spring. More acres were claimed and the sod was broken.

Then Mrs. Blackwell's father died, and she and her husband went Back East for the funeral. She stayed to help her mother, while he came back to the farm. Now everyone who had met her knew that she had good breeding, but she wasn't elevated to the rank of nobility until she came back that summer.

Her husband sent Zeb Greer into Menninger to meet her at the station. After all her luggage was secured in the back seat, they headed out on the Buckingham road in the only surrey in Stevens County.

The road passed through some marshy ground, and a cow had gotten stuck in the mud and died before the owner could find it. The odor of the decaying flesh was oppressive that hot August day.

As they passed the carcass, Mrs. Blackwell said, "The defunct bovine is most obnoxious." To which Zeb replied, "Yeah, that cow stinks like hell, don't it."

After they arrived at the farm, Mrs. Blackwell complained to her husband about the coarseness of Zeb's language, and he was fired.

When Zeb told the story in Menninger, some of the people turned against the Blackwells—Zeb was well-liked and a hard worker—but that's the way with aristocrats: they have enemies, too.

Selling off their claim shack, the Blackwells hired a crew to build what became known as the "Great House," which perched on the east side of the "Hill," overlooking all the farms up and down the "Flats," as the valley and the surrounding area became known. At the time and for several years after, the two-and-a-half story affair was the largest house in Stevens County.

The people on the valley floor, beset by dry weather, the occasional tornado, and the frequent blizzards, could look up at the Great House and take heart, willing to face the threats that came with living on the drift prairies if the Blackwells could.

The Yanktonai who used to ride the land after buffalo were no longer a threat, although occasionally a few young men on horseback would stop at a farm house and use sign language to indicate they were hungry, or a family group might be seen in the gullies picking Juneberries or chokecherries.

The prairie wolves were shot off or poisoned.

However, the new farmers faced other threats:

Lightning strikes could turn dried prairie grass into fuel for fires that roared across the flat ground and the hills, pushed by winds that fanned the flames into a living orange monster that consumed crops, buildings, animals, and the unwary human. It didn't take long for the newcomers to plow fire breaks around their fields and homesteads.

Hail storms chewed up the wheat, barley, oats, and flax, sometimes leaving desolation a mile wide and ten miles long.

Gophers proliferated with the new grain fields as food. While the bounty of a cent a tail enriched the pockets of some small boys, county-provided strychnine was the final solution.

Wheat leaf rust despoiled the yields of some crops by as much as twenty percent, forcing a few farmers out until rust-resistant plants were developed.

Drought wilted the crops, and the dried fields saw auction sales and broken men and their wives leave for a more compassionate environment.

Dark, undulating clouds descended on the grain and revealed themselves as grasshoppers, or locusts to the more Biblically-oriented, which ate anything green or golden. The insects would then turn to weeds. Some buildings even lost their paint to the busy mandibles.

Perseverance is a virtue, but some of the settlers lost their virtue after two or three years of crop failures. Sometimes the Blackwells persuaded them to stay on a little while longer, but sometimes a new family would come in from the East and take over the abandoned farm, or sometimes the Blackwells would buy the land and add it to their own.

Time drifted by; the settlers adapted to the land and the weather; the soil, broken by the plow, grudgingly provided a living for those strong or stubborn enough to stay.

A frame church, serving all denominations, except the Catholics, was erected by the neighborhood men a few miles outside Buckingham. A one-room school house soon joined it. But the Great House was the real center of the community.

Dancing parties; card parties; celebrations on Harvest Home, Thanksgiving, Christmas, New Years; and dances in the huge barn, the largest in the county. Life was good.

Then Charlotte was pregnant.

For months no one saw her, except her husband; Dr. Ramsey; Maggie, the hired girl; and Mrs. Slocum, who would act as midwife. Rumor, probably coming from Maggie, had it that Mrs. Blackwell was not doing well: physically she was fine, but emotionally she had withdrawn, spending many of her waking hours staring out at the valley.

That changed when she went into labor: she became a wild woman, screaming she didn't want the baby. Maggie, Mrs. Slocum, and Edward had to hold her down.

The delivery went well and was almost over when Dr. Ramsey arrived. Mrs. Slocum had everything well in hand.

At first Charlotte refused to see the baby until her husband held her in his arms and assured her that their son was perfect. When she saw little Edward, she burst into tears and thanked God.

Charlotte's mother had passed away, but her two sisters were sent for.

They stayed for several months—both of them were sponsors at the christening—and then returned to New York. When they held little Edward, their bemused looks said they were relieved he was so perfect, but also astonished at his perfection.

It was also rumored that in their self-imposed spinsterhood they were jealous of Charlotte. Their parting at the depot was a mixture of warm hugs and cold looks.

Little Edward was the baby prince of the valley. The farm families all made their obeisance, the men congratulating the proud father, the women making baby clothes and blankets, afraid they weren't good enough. The Blackwells accepted everything with aristocratic dignity, tinged with grateful warmth.

Little Edward flourished. A Ladies Aid society was formed, and he became their unofficial mascot, attending every meeting with his mother. He walked at nine months and was talking, at least his mother said so, at a year.

Buckingham was not going to get its railroad, but the village still tried to challenge the growing town of Menninger. A baseball team was formed with the financial help of the Blackwells, and a power-hitting centerfielder was imported from Chicago. He was a "ringer," of course, but all the small towns—Menninger, Caseyville, Divide, Fishtown—had their own.

A game was scheduled between the two towns on the Fourth of July at the annual Early Pioneers' Picnic at South Finger Lake. Edward and his hired men laid out the diamond.

Over three thousand people brought their picnic baskets and appetites to the grove near the lake. At 2 P.M. the game began, each team playing for pride, but lusting after the hundred-dollar purse.

With the Buckingham "ringer" at bat in the fourth inning, a puppy ran past the Blackwell family sitting on their blanket down the left field line. Little Edward was off like a shot. "Puppeee! Puppeee!" The dog ran down the third base line, Little Edward running after him with his arms outstretched and Edward in pursuit.

The "ringer" was determined to bring the runner on second base home, so he smashed the ball, trying to pull it deep to left, but his timing was slightly off and he ripped a line drive foul instead. The ball caught Little Edward on the temple; he was dead before his body hit the ground.

The picnic was over. Many of the people trailed the Blackwell's buggy to the Hill and stood outside in attendance at the death of a prince.

Charlotte had collapsed into inconsolable tears and was carried to her bedroom. The reverently quiet early evening air was occasionally shattered by the hopeless skirling that interrupted her weeping. The men outside began to fidget and eventually were able to induce their wives to leave for home. What could they do?

She and Edward sat quietly with impassive faces at the funeral. They were very dignified at the committal and in the receiving of condolences from their friends and neighbors. The little boy was buried on the north edge of the Hill, and soon a white stone with a lamb and "Edward" carved on it was placed at the head of the grave. Travelers on the Buckingham road would often see Charlotte sitting beside the stone, rocking herself back and forth with her arms together, but cradling nothing.

The Great House ceased to be the center of the community. Happy times and festive occasions were celebrated in other homes, the church, or a little later in the new and larger township hall.

Edward lost himself in his work and in ironing out difficulties in the community; Charlotte appeared just lost.

On the rare occasions the couple came into Menninger, Edward would talk with the businessmen and farmers, but Charlotte bought what she needed without wasting any words.

The Great War began in Europe, sparked by an assassination that barely rated the front page. While the war destroyed lives and property on an unprecedented scale in Europe, it forced farm prices up in the United States. Flush times: the farmers in the valley expanded their crop land, bought more machinery, and went deeper into debt.

The Blackwells seemed content to pass over into a stolid middle age, but then it was quietly whispered about that Charlotte was pregnant. Neither Maggie nor Mrs. Slocum would confirm or deny the rumors, but some of the women who saw Charlotte in church or shopping or at a social were certain new life was stirring under the loose-waisted hobble skirts or flowing tea gowns she wore. The tongues wagged even more when Charlotte stopped appearing in public and remained in seclusion for several months.

Various busybodies had been counting down the days until the time they expected Charlotte's lying-in, but eventually even the most liberal estimate passed and there was no public appearance of mother and baby. In fact, Charlotte was not seen in the community at all, even though Edward continued with his farming. When people asked about Charlotte, he would look down or off into space and say she was all right. No one dared push the issue, although some rumor started that obviously she was dead, maybe in childbirth, maybe under more sinister circumstances.

Some changes were noted. Maggie started putting on airs: she seemed to have quite a bit of money to buy stylish clothes for the dances and socials, and she was not acting like the deferential servant girl she had been. The Slocums started farming a half-section of good valley land that had belonged to the Blackwells, and no one could figure out how they had gotten the money to buy it. Someone checked the records at the county register of deeds office and found out they had paid exactly one dollar. What was going on?

Edward continued to prosper as a farmer, but he rarely smiled and never laughed, and when the Great Influenza Pandemic spread to Stevens County, he was carried off, along with almost fifty million other human beings worldwide.

Mourners at his funeral were surprised at how Charlotte had aged in the three years of her private isolation.

She had Edward buried on the Hill, beside his son, and people began to notice her kneeling or sitting between the two graves, but she never acknowledged the passing of any wagons, buggies, or, more and more frequently, automobiles.

Charlotte had to take over the running of the farm, so she hired John Amundsen as a foreman and would confer with him on crops, seeding, harvesting, buying, selling, machinery, animals, and the other details of farming activity. She let him know that she was in charge and he was to carry out what she thought best. They conferred in the kitchen, usually at a table with a pot of coffee and some Maggie-baked confection, but he never was invited into the living room.

A light continually shown from the windows of the top half-floor of the big house. No one knew why, and Maggie and the Slocums would only say that Charlotte wanted it that way and change the subject.

The Great War ended; prices eventually fell as peace descended on Europe and cropland there returned to production. The United States suffered an economic downturn, and the farmers were among those who suffered the most.

Some of the valley settlers had overextended and were forced to sell out. Auctions signaled the end of shattered dreams. In the past the Blackwells would buy the land of the failed, but Charlotte was feeling the pinch of low prices as much as anyone, and the land went to some other valley farmer or to total strangers who moved in and saw Charlotte, not as a former community leader and benefactor, but as a strange old woman who lived in the big house on the highway, a house rapidly showing its age.

Foremen came and went, none of them as good as Amundsen. She relied more and more on Mr. Slocum for advice, but he had his own farm to manage.

It was Mrs. Slocum who finally persuaded Charlotte that it would be a good thing for her to become active in the community again.

She started by going to church more regularly; the Slocums would stop by for her. She started going to socials and even allowed Mrs. Slocum to plan a few in her own home. When the social was a family affair, she allowed the little children to scamper and play anywhere in the house, as long as they held on tight to the railings when they went up and down the stairs. No one could get to the attic since the door was padlocked.

At one of the socials Ben Whitman, a bachelor farmer with a lot of land extending from the Divide River Valley to the Finger Lakes, got her to dance. It was apparent to people that she enjoyed it: she and Edward had made a wonderful couple on the dance floor.

Soon at every social it was Ben and Charlotte together; he was very attentive. In the spring before it got too hot, people would see them in a buggy, driving around his land and her land, talking and laughing. It wouldn't be long before the two farms became one, people were certain.

And then it was over.

Speculation as to the why ranged from his rather ungainly girth, to his habitual tobacco chewing, and on to his frequent use of "ain't," and his overbearing mother. Still...there seemed to be something else.

In the heat of July, John Slocum suffered a stroke. After his recovery, his left side was impaired. He could still walk with a cane, but his grasp wasn't good. His farming days were over.

Friends harvested and threshed his crops. In early November the hired man drove John and Cora Slocum and Charlotte to Menninger.

At the depot the ladies sat in their Waiting Room, talking amid occasional tears. When John and Charlotte said goodbye, observers were aware of a genuine affection. Charlotte and Cora shared a long sorrowful embrace, just before Cora followed her husband into the passenger car.

The locomotive chuffed the train into motion. Charlotte was alone in the world.

The Slocums rented out their land while they lived in Pasadena. Cora and Charlotte exchanged letters on a regular basis for a couple years before John's death. After that, it was Easter and Christmas.

Charlotte took on the farm management herself and reduced the number of hired men. The poor years continued. The paint began cracking and flaking off the sides of the Great House. The red barn faded into brown. More of the pioneers got out; the newcomers had no real sense of the old community.

Buckingham passed away. The blacksmith had been gone for years; then the post office was closed. The store burned down. When the minister left, the church folded—no one wanted to serve such an isolated rural parish. The township hall remained, but was used only a couple times a year.

Without Cora, Charlotte grew ever more isolated. She never left her yard; a hired man went to town for supplies. No one came to call.

One Saturday Al Reynolds, one of three hired men, had gone to Menninger to get household and farm supplies, but when a firecracker went off under the wagon, the team spooked and by the time they were stopped, a wheel had been torn off. The wagon maker on West Villard worked on it, but it was long past dark before Reynolds turned in at the Great House.

When he knocked at the back door, there was no answer. When he went in, there was no response to his voice. When he searched the main floor, the second floor, and the basement, he found no one. He quickly roused the other hired men, and they set off to contact the neighbors in hopes Charlotte was visiting.

As Jonas Schumway drove by the Great House, Reynolds was just leaving the yard and told him Charlotte was missing. Schumway said he would keep his eyes peeled.

Several miles to the east, he wasn't thinking of Charlotte anymore. A bachelor, he had become a good cook and a piece of home-made apple pie was waiting for him.

As he started up an incline where many centuries before overflow from the Divide River had rushed southward during heavy releases of water from a large glacial lake several hundred miles to the northwest, he saw something white in the ditch ahead. At first, he thought it was a ghost and then a sheep. Not being afraid of either ghosts or sheep, he hopped down and walked into the ditch. As he got closer, he could see it was a woman all in white and still as death. A suitcase lay beside her. When he turned her face to the moonlight, he saw it was Charlotte and she was still breathing. She said one word: "June."

Back in the Great House, some of the neighbor ladies removed her wedding dress, put her to bed, and opened the suitcase she had with her. It only contained three items: a wedding picture, a little boy's coat, and a pink sleeping garment recognized as the work of Cora Slocum.

When the doctor arrived, he concluded she had nothing physically wrong. After making arrangements for a couple women to stay with her, he left, but returned the next day with the other two members of the County Insanity Board. The three men made a preliminary examination, but it was very limited because Charlotte was unresponsive, although she seemed to be aware of their presence.

A week later they returned and after consulting with her caretakers, concluded that she was legally insane and committed her to the State Asylum in Kingston.

Over the next week papers were signed and attempts were made to contact her relatives in New York, but her sisters had died, and none of the Blackwells could be located. The Bank of Menninger, which had carried the farm debt for several years, took over the farm.

Charlotte never realized the fate of her farm. After the commitment papers were signed, Sheriff James Thorpe and his wife Edna came out to take her to Kingston. However, when the couple attempted to get her into the automobile, Charlotte became hysterical. She kept calling, "June! June!" That name didn't signify anything, but one of the neighbor ladies said Charlotte had never ridden in an auto before; in fact, she had always adamantly refused whenever a ride was offered.

The old buggy was still in a corner of the barn. Al Reynolds hitched up a team. Charlotte had insisted that horses be kept on the property and even had them used for a little plowing and hauling, which she enjoyed watching.

Clothed in her finest dress and with a large out-of-date hat to protect her face from the sun, Charlotte was helped into the buggy. She was still a fine-looking lady.

The buggy and the sheriff's car slowly made their way on the Buckingham road to Menninger. Word got out of their approach, so that when the buggy climbed the hill from the bridge and into town, the streets were lined by several hundred people.

Charlotte paid them no attention. She sat erect, looking neither left nor right. At the Northern Pacific depot, she allowed herself to be helped onto the platform and escorted into the Ladies' Waiting Room by the sheriff's wife. Several dozen people waited outside until the southbound rolled to a stop. Charlotte, her two escorts, and a half dozen other passengers boarded, and that was the last time the great lady was ever seen in Menninger.

Her time in the Asylum was mercifully short; within a year of her confinement, she was dead.

She was never aware of the shock that rippled throughout the county after the authorities went through the Great House.

Nothing in the cellar or the two main floors was any different than what would have been found in a normal farm house. That couldn't be said of the attic.

First, the padlock had to be removed, then Sheriff Thorpe, his wife, and the attorney representing the bank entered the single room, which was mostly empty. Some light coming in the south windows revealed a few pieces of furniture.

The sheriff turned on the single-bulb ceiling light, and the three began looking through a chest of drawers. It was filled with pink sleeping garments in various sizes up to the one found in Charlotte's suitcase. A cedar chest contained a dozen blankets and other bedding. Several sheets of thin rubber were stacked on a shelf.

The sheriff had a flashlight, and it showed a rocking chair with the cushions sunken in as if someone had sat for countless hours rocking back and forth. A large Bible lay on a small table. On the wall a calendar read June 1915.

The men stepped over to a very large wooden crib which they recognized as the unmistakable work of John Slocum.

Their admiration for the wood work turned to horror when they looked into the crib itself. When Mrs. Thorpe approached, she screamed and bolted for the door. Heading down the stairs, she started to wretch. The attorney ran past and headed out for his vehicle. Thorpe stopped and helped his wife out to the porch before he went back in and phoned the County Court House.

When Doc Lee, the County Coroner; a nurse; and Deputy Sheriff Herb Olsen arrived, the men went upstairs, while the nurse comforted Mrs. Thorpe.

Twenty minutes later they emerged, carrying something wrapped in a blanket. They put it in the sheriff's car and Thorpe and Lee got in. Mrs. Thorpe refused to ride in that vehicle, so she went with Olsen and the nurse.

On the way to Menninger, the coroner told the sheriff what seemed to him to be a rational re-creation of what the scene in the attic meant.

Charlotte, indeed, had been pregnant. The delivery must have been a difficult one—the head being presented was extremely large; maybe a call to a doctor was contemplated, but it was never put through. Somehow the birth took place. Charlotte was probably no longer conscious.

The child, if that was what it was, had a body covered by hair, except for the feet, hands and head. The head was at least twice the size of what was normal—it wasn't classical hydrocephaly, but it was a condition of enlargement that had damaged nerve bundles in the brain, with death ensuing in six to eight years, perhaps a little longer. There was no chance of any remission or recovery. That was a fact, not just his opinion.

The Blackwells made a decision: the pregnancy had never been acknowledged, so the delivery was easily hushed up. Mr. Slocum built a crib and it went in the attic. Mrs. Slocum and Charlotte made sleeping garments and took care of the bedding. Rubber sheeting was in place to protect the mattress. Charlotte became as much of a mother as she could, perhaps even nursing her daughter, who was probably not expected to live.

However, years went by; Mrs. Slocum apparently spelled off the exhausted Charlotte in rocking and caring for the child.

The summer's heat, the winter's chill under the un-insulated roof came and went, but the child lived on—fed, changed, rocked, put to sleep, never any variation in the routine. What were Charlotte's thoughts as she held her daughter close to her heart? Did she love her? She couldn't have any hopes for her. The one emotion she probably had was fear, fear of discovery.

The child's body and head kept growing, but there was no mental or emotional growth, no real personality. Then about the age of ten, the child died. It was summertime.

There was probably a discussion as to what to do with the body. It couldn't be buried in a grave seen by the public. Evidently, someone wouldn't allow a secret burial. Time passed. The stifling attic heated by an unsympathetic sun and the remains, shut up, perhaps for months, were mummified.

After that someone—it could only have been Charlotte—would rock with the body, put it back in the crib, and continued to do that for many years as attested by the worn-out sleeping garments.

Then the routine was shattered. On the last day as Charlotte held the body over the crib, the head fell off. The shock caused Charlotte to drop the body in a contorted position on the mattress. Perhaps she was screaming, perhaps praying, whatever she was doing, the strain of the years in the attic were quickly taking their toll. Before she left her daughter behind for the last time, she had collected one of the sleeping garments and secured the padlock. She went to her closet, put on her wedding dress, packed her suitcase, and in the coroner's opinion, "headed for home."

His subsequent examination of the body did not cause him to change any of his opinions. He did add to his report that the body hair was like the fur of a bear.

Charlotte's remains were taken to the Eternal Rest Cemetery north of Menninger, where they were interred beside those of her husband and son, who had been reburied there. Next to Charlotte was her daughter. Her body had been interred over the protests of some who claimed she was not human. The name on her daughter's stone read, "June." Her daughter didn't care.

Money from the sale of the farm allowed for a large granite gravestone with "Blackwell" carved on it. the Blackwells didn't care.

The Great House was allowed to disintegrate. It had the reputation of being haunted, and no woman wanted to live there. Wind tore off the shutters and some of the shingles. Rain and snow brought more destruction. Neighbors who hadn't known the Blackwells began ripping off pieces of the house to fix up their own. No one cared.

No one even cared when a fire destroyed what remained of the Great House.

A minor dispute arose in the Menninger Ladies' Cemetery Auxiliary when its president demanded the name of the cemetery be changed to Eternal Peace. Eventually, the name change occurred because of the work she had done for the organization, but four members in the opposition resigned in protest.

When the cemetery sign was changed to Eternal Peace, none of the dead cared.

THE BARITONE AND THE SAVIOR

M y father had a wonderful baritone voice, but he stopped singing in church the Sunday after Congress declared war on Germany.

We lived on a farm southeast of Menninger, North Dakota, which was actually the Scandinavian side, mostly Norwegians, some Swedes, Brits, Scots, and some shanty Irish from the Auld Sod. West of Menninger was where most of the Germans lived, with an occasional outlier like an Englishman or Irishman mixed in.

The west-side Germans were mostly Roman Catholic, and the families generally had an origin in southern Germany. Since they did a lot of their business in Menninger, which had a Catholic church, they went to Mass there, but as soon as the village of Cologne was platted on the new Carver Cut-off of the Great Northern, the west-side Germans built their own church, St. Bruno of Cologne. The city of Cologne wasn't in southern Germany, more in the west, but the people in that part of Germany were anti-Prussian, as they were in the southern part, plus one of the big west-side farmers had relatives back in Cologne, so that name was chosen.

We east-side Germans had relatives in northern Germany, but none were among the powerful Junker families in Prussia. The Junkers had sided with Martin Luther, for the most part, so we didn't hate them the way the southern Germans did. Most of us east-siders were Lutherans, so even though the Catholics in Menninger were mostly German and some Irish, we didn't go to church there.

Beginning in the late 1880s, a Lutheran minister had a circuit of three congregations—Menninger and two to the south—and that continued until after the turn of the century when we decided it was time for a building, instead of meeting in one of the Lodge halls. A couple lots were purchased on Dunnell Avenue, and the men of the congregation did a lot of the carpentry work themselves, building a wood-frame church with a steeple.

When it came time for the dedication, invitations went out to other congregations. Many Congregationalists, Baptists, and Methodists helped us celebrate, but not a single Catholic, not even a German one.

Germany was a relatively new nation; a Junker, Otto von Bismarck, had united the disparate German States through a policy of "blood and iron." That meant war with Denmark, then Austria, and finally France, and out of their defeats arose the German Empire in 1871. When Germany was born, the United States was already ninety-five years old.

It took awhile, but eventually most German-speakers accepted the unification. Those who emigrated to North Dakota were thrilled to discover the name of the state capital was Bismarck, a new nation's pride and all that.

Besides language, something else united us—beer. Whether the summer picnics were held in a grove west or east of Menninger, the wives and daughters brought huge amounts of food—sausages, cabbage, noodles from the east-siders; boiled potatoes, rye bread, blood sausage, from the west; and sauerkraut with roast pork or sausages and dumplings from everyone. Some men from the west side also brewed coffee in large coffee pots set on a grill right over the flames.

Even though it was illegal in North Dakota, the men also produced large containers of beer—dark beers and lagers from the east side, and pale lagers and pilsners from the west-siders, who also sneaked in some schnapps. Some of the older farmers had elaborate brewing systems in their barns, the smell masked by the odor of animals and manure. The sheriff and his deputies always looked the other way. If they were

German, they also had a taste of the home-brew before averting their eyes.

Religion was the dividing factor: the west-siders were loyal to the Pope, and we were just as strong for Martin Luther. So strong, in fact, that when they built a Norwegian Lutheran Church in town, the adults in our church were scandalized that such a liberal interpretation of Lutheran doctrine had sprung up so close to their children and grandchildren. All those cold days and nights in Norway must have frozen the true faith out of the Lutherans' brains.

It didn't help matters when the size of the Norwegian Lutheran congregation surpassed us within two years.

All the religious division made me feel bad that most Christians in the Menninger area had never heard the Jansen twins and their older brother Karl-Otto sing in a church setting. When Elisabeth, Emma, and Karl-Otto sang in our church, their blended voices made it almost seem as if three angels had come to inspire us.

The Jansen family lived on a farm three miles from us, so I knew the kids even though they were all older than I was. The girls sang in church as a duet—Elisabeth was a soprano and Emma was an alto—until Karl-Otto's voice changed, then he began joining them at Christmas and Easter. While the girls would sing together at socials and at talent shows, Karl-Otto never sang outside our church.

Music is a great unifier, and I truly believe that for three years our congregation was strengthened by that trio as much as by anything Rev. Schneider preached about. "O Holy Night," "Silent Night," "Christ Jesus Lay in Death's Strong Bands," and "Jesus Christ Is Risen Today" were my favorites.

Then came the great division, born among European conflicts, pride, and fear. With the creation of a united Germany and, a year earlier, Italy, the already established monarchies, along with the French Republic, saw potential enemies to their cultures and empires.

Eventually, European strength gravitated into two camps created through secret alliances: Germany, Austria-Hungary, and Italy formed the Triple Alliance, while Great Britain, France, and Russia established the Triple Entente.

Although the nations in each alliance were supposed to work together, each of them, plus many smaller countries such as Serbia, maintained a strong sense of nationalistic fervor. In fact, the Austro-Hungarian Empire was a hotbed for rabid nationalistic groups.

The two alliance systems built huge fighting forces, both land and naval power.

While Britain, France, and Russia had well-established empires, they looked askance at similar colony-acquisitions by the Germans and Italians and tried to block any such attempts. Russia also looked at the Ottoman Empire as an enemy.

Europe teetered on the brink and then in June 1914 the assassination of Austrian Archduke Franz Ferdinand and his wife Sophie in Sarajevo by a Serbian nationalist, pushed Europe over the edge. The alliance system pulled the major powers into conflict, with the exception of the Italians, who begged off, saying they were only obligated to help the Germans and Austrians in a defensive war. The guns fired in August sounded the death knell for European peace and the start of the Great War.

That same month President T. Woodrow Wilson pledged American neutrality and his service as a mediator which suited the tenor of the country, not just the German-Americans; however, as the war dragged on, he began to side more with Great Britain and the Allies, which really upset my father.

In 1915 Germany declared the waters around the British Isles and Ireland a "war region." Any ships found in those waters would be subject to being stopped and searched or sunk. A little over a week later the *William P. Frye*, an American ship hauling wheat to England, was sunk by a German cruiser off the coast of Brazil. In May a German sub torpedoed, but did not sink, the American tanker *Gulflight* off the Scilly Isles. Three American sailors were killed. Then on May 7 the British Cunard liner *Lusitania* was sunk by a torpedo off the coast of Ireland with 124 American lives lost.

It was very difficult for us German-Americans to defend such actions, but our fatherland, Germany was fighting for its existence.

In July Wilson had his War and Navy departments begin work on a defense program. Rumors were rampant about German espionage and sabotage in American munitions factories, then the American steamer *Leelanaw* was torpedoed.

On August 19 the Star liner *Arabic* was torpedoed off Ireland; two Americans died. Eight days later the German Navy stated that on September 1 its ships would cease attacking passenger ships without warning in a futile attempt to cool American anger over the submarine attacks on non-military vessels.

That month the United States War College Division tried to squelch stories in the *Washington Post* and the *Baltimore Sun* that the U.S. was planning on sending a million soldiers to help the Allies.

On October 12 Edith Cavell, an English nurse, was shot by the Germans for helping British prisoners escape from Belgium to neutral Holland. American public opinion was inflamed even more against Germany. Two days later the U.S. Congress agreed to increase the size of the American army.

On December 4 American auto maker Henry Ford sailed to Europe on the "Peace Ship," *Oscar II*. We hoped that he and the friends who accompanied him would be successful and stop the senseless killing, but the press ridiculed his efforts and the mission was a failure.

The next year started off very badly for the Germans. The press, most of which sided with Wilson, trumpeted each anti-German story. Rumors of German actions that didn't make the newspapers were shunted along the "German-American telegraph," made up of all the Germans who had settled in the United States from Pennsylvania, along the southern shores of the Great Lakes, and into the interior of Wisconsin, Minnesota, and North Dakota, so we knew things not reported by the press.

On January 15 evidence was produced showing that Von Papen, the German naval attaché to the U.S., was paying German agents operating in the United States.

From January 27 to February 3, Wilson began a nationwide whistle-stop campaign to generate support for American entry into the war. My father and many other German-Americans thought that was completely unfair: the official American policy was neutrality.

On March 1 a desperate Germany began a campaign of unlimited submarine warfare to starve Britain. What else could they do, except surrender and be destroyed?

On March 15 Wilson sent 12,000 soldiers across the Mexican border to chase Pancho Villa; eight airplanes joined the chase on March 19. We knew that Wilson was not as peace-minded as he pretended.

On March 24 a torpedo sank the French cross-channel steamer *Sussex*, killing fifty. On April 19 Wilson called on Germany to stop sinking non-military ships without warning. Germany complied the next day, and on May 4 Germany made the "*Sussex* Pledge" to stop sinking merchant ships without warning. Germany was walking a tightrope: if too many ships got through, England would become more powerful and win the war; if more were sunk, Wilson would take England's side.

On April 12 a plot to blow up American munitions ships by German agents was revealed. How could we say that was acceptable?

On April 27 British Secretary of War, Marshal Lord Kitchener, asked the U.S. to join the war and send troops to Europe.

On June 3 the National Defense Act authorized a five-year expansion of the American army.

On July 30 suspected German saboteurs blew up a munitions plant at Black Tom Island, NY.

In 1916 Wilson ran against the Republican Charles Evans Hughes under the slogan "He Kept Us Out of War." None of us German-Americans could argue with that statement, and many voted for Wilson, who won with 277 electoral votes to 254 for Hughes. Wilson even took traditionally Republican North Dakota by 1735 votes, although he had also won the state in 1912 in a three-man race, becoming the first Democrat to carry North Dakota.

On December 12 Germany offered a "Peace Note," saying she was not responsible for the war and would agree to stop fighting if she could keep all the territory gained.

On December 20 Wilson asked for "Peace Notes" from all the belligerent nations; this offended the British because it sounded as if Wilson equated their war aims with the "immoral" aims of Germany. On December 26 Germany responded and asked for a peace conference.

spiked helmet and carrying a rifle, dragging a poor innocent girl off to be ravished; the background was flames), billboards, songs, speakers, all intoned a hatred of everything German. German soldiers were supposed to have "pitchforked" Belgian babies with their bayonets. They were alleged to have plucked out the eyeballs of civilians and filled a bathtub with them and hacked the breasts off Belgian women.

Fourteen states forbade the teaching of German in schools. At the Menninger High School three languages were taught: English, Latin, and German. After the declaration of war, German was banned. Sauerkraut was renamed "Liberty cabbage," hamburgers were "Liberty sausage," dachshunds became "Liberty dogs," German measles were known as "Liberty measles." In several locales German immigrants were forced to kneel, spit on the German flag, kiss the Stars and Stripes, and yell, "To Hell with the Kaiser." In Illinois a German immigrant was lynched.

In every way possible Germans were demonized; they became devils.

Luckily, the people in and around Menninger recognized us as good people, and except for the dismissal of German from the school curriculum and a few snide comments, we rode out the war without being deemed Satan's helpers.

On April 28 Congress passed the Army bill allowing for a draft; on April 30 Germany announced that all ships in the war zone were targets; on May 18 Wilson signed the Selective Service Act; on May 26 the first U.S. troops reached France.

June 5, 1917, was draft registration day. All men from twenty-one to thirty-one were required to register. There were exemptions for married registrants with dependents and low incomes, state and federal government officials, the clergy, convicted felons, and those medically, mentally, or morally unfit.

Only two German-Americans around Menninger failed to register. One was found hiding in the hayloft of his family's barn and decided he would rather register than face prison. The other was never found. The supposition was he headed to the Encampment, a group of non-conformists and outlaws who lived as a law unto themselves in the hills west of Caseyville, which was sixteen miles south of Menninger. If you walked in a straight line from most of the west-side German farms, you'd hit the Encampment.

On June 15 Wilson signed the Espionage Act. It banned actions that interfered with the war effort. Most of us German-Americans found no fault with it. A nation must survive.

Almost a year later, on May 16, 1918, despite opposition from former president Theodore Roosevelt and Senators Henry Cabot Lodge of Massachusetts and Hiram Johnson of California, the Sedition Act was enacted. It made illegal any utterance of disloyalty about the American government, the flag, or the military that would turn public opinion against such institutions. Any dissent in the German-American communities around Menninger was blunted.

On June 25 members of the U.S. 1st Division began landing in France; on July 20 the drawing of draft numbers began; on October 24 the 1st Division fired its first shots of the war near the Swiss border; on November 3 the first Americans, twenty in all, were killed in the war.

It wasn't until September 5 that the first contingent of Stevens County men, two members of Company B of the North Dakota 2nd Regiment, left for Camp Dodge in Iowa. On September 19 the second group left, escorted by the band; a third group left on October 3. Karl-Otto was among the latter.

When the 2nd Regiment arrived in Camp Greene, North Carolina, it was disbanded and became part of the 41st Division, which soon moved to Camp Mills, New York. When they landed in France in December, they were part of the 164th Infantry.

A revolution in Russia pulled that nation out of the war, and Germany began transferring its troops from the Eastern to the Western Front. If not for the arrival of the Americans, the Germans would probably have overwhelmed the British and French and ended the war. As it was, the AEF (American Expeditionary Force), as the army was called, provided the muscle to push the Germans back in a series of battles: Cantigny, Belleau Wood, Second Battle of the Marne, Chateau-Thierry, Saint-Mihiel, and the Meuse-Argonne.

By March casualty reports had begun coming back to Menninger. Names included men from Stevens County, but also some from the neighboring counties of Walters and Dawn.

The terrible initials "KIA" were the signature of Death. They cast a pall of grief over the families and the friends of the dead and surrounded the entire community with a net of sadness. If the man killed in action was a member of your congregation, the death was doubly hard. So it was for us when the name Karl-Otto Jansen appeared in the summer of 1918.

Karl-Otto had been killed during a German counterattack at the Battle of Cantigny. He and some other privates of the 164th had been transferred to the 1st Battalion of the 26th Infantry, 1st Division, commanded by Theodore Roosevelt, Jr. The counterattack was driven back, but Karl-Otto would never sing again. He and three other soldiers were in a shell hole when a high explosive shell from a German howitzer blew them into pieces so small they could not be identified.

The Jansens didn't have anyone buried in Eternal Rest Cemetery north of Menninger. And now they wouldn't even have Karl-Otto. I'd seen other families and my own folks stand beside a grave, bow their heads, and pray or meditate or think. Sometimes I'd see people crying. I felt sorry for the Jansens, having no piece of earth to enfold Karl-Otto, except some hole in France no one would ever remember.

Elisabeth and Emma were home from college for the summer, but they never sang in our church. Many Sundays I'd see them in quiet tears. That fall they went back to college. And then at 11 A.M. on Monday, November 11, 1918, the Great War ended.

But that didn't end the conflicts.

I thought everything would go back to normal. Germany would be punished, sure, but not humiliated. German-Americans would stop being looked upon as potential traitors. My father would forgive Wilson and become an even better American.

On Christmas Eve I was certain of it.

At our service with the decorated Christmas tree, the little bags of candy and nuts and apples for the children under it, the relief everyone felt at having our first six weeks of peace, there was more rejoicing, feelings of good cheer, and honoring of the Christ Child and His spirit of love than anyone had displayed for years.

There was some sorrow, also, as we remembered Karl-Otto and the other twenty-four men who did not return to the homes they had left some fifteen months before. When the Jansen twins and their parents came in, that feeling was multiplied.

I think we were all surprised when Rev. Schneider announced that Elisabeth and Emma were going to sing. They hadn't done any singing since Karl-Otto went into the army.

When they began "O Holy Night," I had to put my head down and stare at my shoes. I remembered how Karl-Otto's baritone filled out the power of the hymn, and I knew if I looked up and didn't see him, my eyes would leak tears.

Then, suddenly, there was a male voice, a baritone, that provided a harmony allowing the higher voices to soar above our world and bear witness to the spirit of Jesus Christ, the Savior.

I looked up: there was my father. My eyes winked wet.

The trio also sang "Silent Night" in German—"Stille Nacht, Heilige Nacht…." After that eyes were going wet all over the place, and some women and girls were actually sobbing. It was what I would call profound.

After that, even the distribution of the children's gifts was anti-climactic.

The girls didn't sing that Sunday, and by the next Sunday they had returned to college.

My father didn't sing, either, but I thought he soon would: the war was over.

I was wrong.

I hadn't counted on the depths the Allies would go to humiliate Germany: Great Britain, France, and Japan sitting like lions around a prostrate Germany, tearing off chunks of German territory, demanding huge sums of money, pouring disgrace and humiliation on the heads of the German people, with Australia, New Zealand, Belgium, South Africa, and Portugal playing the role of jackals by picking up a few stray pieces, and the new nations of Poland and Czechoslovakia dropping in like vultures and grabbing some fragments, even though they had not been Allies.

The British were rabid about making Germans "pay," not just in money, but in lives. The British Navy maintained its wartime blockade of German ports and forbade the German fishing fleet access to the Baltic Sea, where the German populace had obtained needed food throughout the war. Most Germans were victims of chronic malnutrition; in northern Germany eight hundred adults per day starved to death. The French backed their British allies: Clemenceau remarked, "There are twenty million Germans too many." The Italian leadership was of the same ghoulish frame of mind.

In January, February, and March of 1919, tens of thousands of Germans were allowed to starve to death. Eight-year old German children weighed as much as a five-year old American child. Rickets puffed out their foreheads; edema swelled their hungry stomachs.

In December 1918 Wilson and his advisers sailed for France aboard the *George Washington* to make a treaty. More than thirty Allied nations met in Paris. Twenty-seven nations helped prepare reports, but basically the Big Five controlled the conference and its agenda: the United States, Great Britain, France, Italy, and Japan.

Russia was excluded because she had signed a peace treaty with Germany in March 1918. None of the Central Powers, including Germany, were allowed representation, even though they hadn't been occupied and had not surrendered unconditionally.

Japan wanted some German-controlled islands in the South Pacific and once she got them, her diplomats were ready to return home, leaving the Big Four in charge.

Italy had signed a secret treaty with Great Britain and France, guaranteeing her certain areas in Europe controlled by Austria-Hungary and a port in Turkey after the war. The other members of the Big Four agreed to give Italy part of Trentino, the port of Zara, and the Dalmatian islands, but would not give her part of the Tyrol, the Istria peninsula, the city of Valona in Albania, the vital Adriatic ports of Trieste and Fiume, or the Dalmatian coast. The Italian Prime Minister Vittorio Orlando flew into a rage: Did not the Italian people lose 500,000 soldiers and another 500,000 civilians due to malnutrition and disease, plus countless treasure? First, he suffered a nervous breakdown, then he left the conference. Now it was a Big Three.

Georges Clemenceau, the French premier, hated all things German. France had suffered huge losses in the war and he was out for revenge: he would emasculate Germany and ensure she would never threaten France again. France would take the Rhineland as a buffer between his country and Germany. France would take the Saar, depriving Germany of much of its industrial base of coal and iron. The provinces of Alsace and Lorraine would be returned to France (Germany had taken them in 1871) even though the majority of residents spoke German. The German colonies in West Africa—Togoland and Cameroon—would become French. Germany must vastly reduce her army. And Germany must pay huge reparations for all the war damage France had suffered. His nickname was "Le Tigre" ("The Tiger"), and he deserved it after ripping Germany to shreds at the conference.

Great Britain's Prime Minister David Lloyd George wished to support his French ally in the quest to make Germany impotent. He backed France's demands for reparations, control of portions of the German homeland, and the reduction of the German army, but he also pushed for the reduction of the German navy. When it came to the German colonies, Lloyd George was right in there chewing: Great Britain got the major share of German East Africa (renamed Tanganyika), but Belgium and Portugal were each allowed to bite off a piece.

The Allies also split Germany into two parts by taking a strip of land ("the Polish Corridor") and giving it to Poland, so that newly recreated nation would have access to the Baltic Sea. The Corridor separated the bulk of Germany from East Prussia, and German citizens passing between the two were treated like aliens.

When Wilson arrived, he was the first sitting American president to visit Europe; he was also a savior, at least in his own eyes. He had saved America by increasing the power of the national government under his program ironically called the "New Freedom," which entailed a new anti-trust act, the Federal Reserve System, the Federal Trade Commission, the Federal Farm Loan Act, the 16th Amendment (a federal income tax), the 17th amendment (direct election of U.S. Senators), and a host of other laws which sapped strength from the states, private businesses, and private citizens in order to empower the federal government even more. Wilson could not be a king, but he could exercise close-to royal power as a benevolent democrat.

He was certainly the most idealistic of the Big Four leaders. He came riding in on the Fourteen Points, based on a speech he'd made the previous year. Under that banner the United States would push for no more secret alliances, freedom of the seas, free trade, reduction of armaments, an adjustment of colonial claims, the self-determination of ethnic groups, and a League of Nations. After the conference Lloyd George said he thought he hadn't done too badly for England despite the fact he was seated between Jesus Christ (Wilson) and Napoleon (Clemenceau).

Poor Wilson. Clemenceau and Lloyd George outfoxed him on the major points, but they allowed him to keep his League of Nations and his belief in the self-determination of all peoples. In a final slap in the face of the German people, Wilson did not oppose Article 231 being placed in the treaty, which blamed the war entirely on Germany and her allies.

Article 231: "The Allied and Associated Governments affirm and Germany accepts the responsibility of Germany and her allies for causing all the loss and damage to which the Allied and Associated Governments and the nationals have been subjected as a consequence of the war imposed upon them by the aggression of Germany and her allies."

Germany signed the Treaty of Versailles on June 28, 1919. She had no choice.

Plain and simple, the Treaty said Germany, its people, and the German government were all guilty of fomenting the war.

Serbian nationalism which caused the death of the Archduke and his wife bore no guilt. Russia bore none of the guilt for urging Serbia to stand up to Austria-Hungary or for the early mobilization of her forces, which caused Germany to mobilize. France bore none of the guilt for not pressuring her ally Russia to stand down, and, in fact, for giving Russia a "blank check" of support.

Much was made of the so-called "blank check" of July 5 and 6, 1914, in which Germany gave support to Austria-Hungary, her ally, for action against Serbia. Supporters of Wilson claimed the support was "unconditional," but opponents said it was conditional in order to minimize conflict in the Balkans. The distinction was never investigated: France's "blank check" was approved; Germany's "blank check" was condemned.

When Wilson had arrived in Europe and traveled in France, England, and Italy, in Brest, Paris, Dover, London, Mentone, Rome, Vatican City, Milan, and Turin, it was like Palm Sunday as thousands cheered him: "Veelson! Veelson!" or "Wilson! Wilson!" depending on their pronunciation of the "W." But when he left for home with his patched-up treaty, he was a dour, unsmiling old man with deteriorating health. He couldn't understand. Why didn't Britain and France accede to all his wishes? His ideas would save the world from another war.

Immediately, he undertook to gain the Senate's approval of the Treaty of Versailles, but the majority of Republicans, fearful that membership in the League of Nations would involve the sons of Americans fighting in Europe again, opposed ratification, as did some Democrats, especially if they were German or Irish Catholic.

Wilson decided to take the issue to the people and on September 3 embarked on a train tour of the western United States, making speeches to drum up support for the Treaty. The President planned to visit every state, but four, west of the Mississippi and be gone for twenty-seven days, riding in his private blue car, the *Mayflower*.

In Bismarck his little party took an auto tour of the city. When they returned to the train, two tramps who had sneaked under a car were flushed out. Wilson shook hands with them before they took off. When my father read that, he smiled, but that was for the tramps, not for Wilson.

Wilson kept up a murderous pace, speaking in the heat of a Western late-summer. His doctor saw him getting weaker day-by-day. Down the Pacific Coast to San Diego, up to Los Angeles, across the mountains, speaking, asking, pleading, for the people's support for his doomed treaty.

Asthma, headaches, sleeplessness. Reno, Ogden, Salt Lake City, Cheyenne, Denver. His triumphal march toward a New Jerusalem.

On September 25 he stumbled through a speech in Pueblo, Colorado, in which he attacked any hyphenated Americans as being ready to plunge a dagger into the vitals of America. We German-Americans, as well as the Irish-Americans and the Italian-Americans, were appalled; my father's hatred of Wilson grew.

That night between Pueblo and Wichita, Kansas, he suffered a stroke: spittle dripped out of the side of his mouth; the left side of his face was paralyzed. He was rushed back to Washington, D.C., in his darkened private car and up to the second floor of the White House. His head felt like it was splitting. As the open automobile in which he rode passed through the almost-deserted streets of the nation's capital, he took off his hat, bowed, and waved, as if he were responding to the huge cheering throngs in Europe all over again.

On October 2 another, more serious, stroke paralyzed his left side, collapsed the left half of his face, and substantially reduced the vision in his right eye. His wife (his second; his first wife died of kidney failure in 1913) and Dr. Cary T. Grayson, his personal physician, cut him off from all visitors, and his wife acted as a filter between him and any government work.

When Senator Lodge made common-cause with some of the Democratic Senators through proposing compromises to be placed in the treaty, Wilson's other-worldly idealism and his precarious health caused him to reject any such compromises, and the treaty went down to defeat in the Senate. Wilson was left with only the 1919 Nobel Peace Prize as a monument to his unyielding ego.

Wilson left office in March 1921, a broken, disillusioned man. He never fully recovered from the effects of the strokes and lived out his life as a partial invalid in a three-story brick house at 2340 S Street, in northwest Washington, D.C.

He passed away in an upstairs bedroom on Sunday, February 3, 1924.

The next Sunday my father sang in church.

DOC BLANCHARD

They tore the Oleson House down in 1970. Before the wrecking crew began their work, the residents of Menninger, many of whom had never been inside, turned out for a last viewing. In a room on the third floor, they saw a cabinet with hundreds of small empty red containers marked "Morphine." Several dozen more were on the floor, knocked off their shelves by the curious. Several dozen more still contained Morphine!—the rumors were true!

After Eric and Lena Oleson built the Oleson House, it commanded the corner of Villard and Dakota for over seventy years even though it was a couple lots east of that corner. Its four-story height towered over the various drugstores, meat markets, cafés, and blacksmith shops (later to become gasoline stations or auto repair shops) that clustered around that end of Menninger, North Dakota, and that made it a landmark… and a destination.

Three governors had stayed there, and one of them used it as his election headquarters for central North Dakota. A United States Congressman had eaten in its dining room. Pronouncing the meal the best fried chicken he'd ever had, he moved aside the large potted plants and stood in the big front window, looking out at the traffic, waving to his constituents, and smoking a black cheroot.

The burning of the large Agnes Hotel on Chicago Street, and the coming of the Great Northern in the form of the Carver Cut-off were temporary reprieves for the Oleson, but then a new brick hotel—the Menninger Arms over on Lamborn—challenged the Oleson and gradually became the number one hotel in town.

A coal furnace and forced-air heat, new furnishings, a revamped menu, a new gray paint job replacing the weather-beaten white, nothing stopped the decline. A motel on the Gold Star Highway and the GN's decision not to change crews in Menninger took away the travelers and the railroad men. Bright orange siding and a bevy of "soiled doves" and their madam were not enough, either.

When Eric passed away from a heart attack after shoveling snow off the front sidewalk, Lena shut the hotel and moved into the rest home on the west side of town. Two years later she was dead.

While the most famous names on the hotel register were those of the governors and the Congressman, Doc Blanchard was the most infamous resident, even more so than Donna Hudson and her "girls."

Dr. Richard Blanchard was a native of Virginia and had retained a slight Southern accent even after his years in a New York medical school. Menninger already had two doctors, so it was difficult to fathom why a young man just starting his practice had chosen Menninger, a lonely town on the prairie. Some Romantics said he had killed a man in a duel over a young lady and was hiding out, but that view was discounted because Doc Blanchard was not a very handsome man, and true Romance needs a good-looking hero that girls and young women can fantasize about.

Luckily for him, there was no competition with the other medical men: they passed some of their cases to him, and when they discovered he had some surgical skill, they asked his assistance on a few of their more complicated cases, an assistance that showed he had an aptitude for the use of the scalpel in some outstanding, even brilliant, operations.

There was no actual hospital in Menninger: some rooms were rented by the doctors in the Oleson for surgery and for recovery. Doc Blanchard lived in the Oleson, so he was the doctor "on call."

After he got to know the town, he began calling on the blind pigs that had set up shop after North Dakota came in "dry," and it became illegal to sell liquor or beer. At first he drank in moderation, but then his intake began to increase as his tolerance level for alcohol grew. He started to run with a crowd that drank, gambled, and made certain to get their friend "Doc" into the Oleson via the back stairs to avoid any public scandal. In the crowd were a dentist, a young lawyer, the newspaper editor, and several businessmen, as well as the usual riff-raff.

About a year after he arrived, Doc was drunk in his bed when there was a knock at the door. A young woman who worked as a servant girl for one of the druggists had developed a severe pain in her right side. The other doctors were not available: one had gone for a visit to his former home in Canada and the other was at a medical convention Fargo.

Doc sent word to Hazel Fink, the crusty woman who worked as his nurse, and while waiting for her, he tried to sober up with black coffee and cold water splashed on his face.

The young woman was taken to the fourth floor where there was a small examining room and a larger operating room. Doc diagnosed appendicitis and the patient was prepped for emergency surgery.

What would have been a piece of cake for Doc sober, turned into a disaster for Doc drunk. While the druggist and his wife waited in the hotel lobby, they talked about how quiet Doc had been, but didn't suspect it was because he was so inebriated.

The lights were not as bright as they should have been, and while the inflamed appendix was removed successfully, Doc sewed the wound without checking thoroughly for hemorrhaging. The young woman was placed in a regular room, Nurse Hazel stayed with her, and Doc went to bed.

In the morning the nurse was alarmed by the pale face that stared up at her. She ran for Doc, who immediately knew he had to operate. It was too late: the abdomen was filled with black blood. The servant girl let out a little gasp and was still. Doc began to cry. The nurse took him to his room before she sent for the undertaker.

The girl's body was sent off to her home in Minnesota, but no one from Menninger attended her funeral, not even the druggist or his wife. After all, she was only a servant.

One good thing did come of the affair—Doc swore off liquor.

He also became a much better doctor, showing much more compassion for his patients than he had previously.

In 1912 T. Woodrow Wilson was elected president, the first Democrat since Grover Cleveland. Wilson, a Progressive, wanted to expand the power of the federal government and got Congress to go along both on domestic issues and on foreign ones what with the deterioration of European peace. Wilson also took the time to invade Nicaragua, Haiti, the Dominican Republic, and Mexico.

In 1916 he ran for re-election on the slogan "He Kept Us Out of War" and won. Five months later he asked the United States Congress to declare war on Germany, which it happily did.

A Selective Service Act was passed the next month, and a farm boy from west of town was called upon to defend his country. The night before he left, he took his best girl for a buggy ride. The stars and the crescent moon were romantic; the grass under the trees where they stopped the buggy was soft; his pleading words overcame her moral resistance.

When it was over, Hannah didn't feel bad; she wanted to do something for the boy who said he loved her and might soon die. Just before he boarded the train the next day, he told her he loved her again. Her heart swelled. Perhaps she loved him, too.

The next month, however, she did feel bad. The "curse" hadn't come.

She waited another month; no "curse." In the mornings she sometimes couldn't clean the rooms in the Oleson where she worked as a chambermaid; her stomach couldn't hold anything down.

Finally, she knocked on the doctor's door. After she told her story through a flood of tears, he said to check with him at the end of the week.

Doc Blanchard agonized his way over the next seventy-two hours. He was a doctor; he wanted to help. As a doctor he had taken an oath to protect life. Was the thing inside the type of life that had to be protected? If it were expelled, it couldn't survive. If he left it alone, it would become a child like those he saw on the streets with their mothers, being carried, cared for, loved. Maybe Hannah would love her child also if he didn't destroy it.

His conscience was so conflicted, he almost went back to the bottle.

The dreaded knock came, and he was surprised to see another young woman, another chambermaid, but at the Hotel Logan across the tracks on St. Paul, ducking her head in shame next to Hannah.

Annika Cronquist's story was the same old "seduced and abandoned" account, but with a variation: the seducer was C.J. Bangs, a bald, portly, traveling cigar salesman that Doc and most of the townspeople thought might be a eunuch since he never paid any attention to women. Doc saw he'd have to rethink his opinion of Bangs, but he knew he couldn't tell anyone why.

When he saw the desperation in Annika's face (her parents were straitlaced Swedish Baptists who rarely got into town from their farm) and the hopeful look on Hannah's face, any mental objections he had, melted away and he told them he'd have something for them in two weeks. Hannah, lost in the joy of the moment, actually hugged Doc; Annika just whispered "Tack" smothered in her Swedish accent as she retreated out the door.

The very next day Doc caught the train to Kingston, hopped on the mainline of the Northern Pacific to the Twin Cities, switched to the Burlington Route to Chicago, boarded the B&O to the nation's capital, took the Atlantic Coast Line to Petersburg, Virginia, and then the Norfolk & Western to Suffolk.

He was home, but he didn't go home, where he was still unwelcome due to a youthful love affair gone wrong. He got a room in a hotel. The next day he hired a rig and headed for the Great Dismal Swamp.

His destination was a wooden shack where the woman lived who'd gotten him out of the dilemma he found himself in after his hormone-induced indiscretion. However, it did cost him his birthright. No one knew her real name, so she was called "Snake Root Annie."

Oh, yes, Annie remembered him. Her smile revealed teeth or the lack of them which showed that time hadn't been kind. He revealed his purpose in coming.

"Ya want what your pappy ordered back in...when was that? Eight-eighty?"

"Eighty-seven."

She cackled. "Good memory, but I guess that's somethin' ya don't ferget so easy."

"No."

"And now ya come back. Ya 'sponsible agin?"

"No."

"I see; ya want my medicine for a fren', huh?"

"Something like that."

"Ya come back tomarr; I'll have somethin' for ya. Blue cohosh, Queen Anne's lace, pennyroyal, and two o' my special charms which no one knows, but me." She winked and the whole side of her face wrinkled. "Not even that fakir woman over on Nine-Mile Creek, damn her eyes. Oh, I fergot, she's only got one." She burst out a laugh.

Doc returned the next day for his package and made arrangements for her to send him more whenever he requested. She told him to order way ahead of when he needed her mixture because she didn't get over to the post office, but twice a month; she didn't like to be stared at.

Back in Menninger Doc waited for the inevitable knock. He was perfectly reconciled to what he was about to do. Someone needed help and that was what a doctor was for.

The knock came, Nurse Hazel was summoned, and all three people climbed the stairs to the fourth floor. Doc readied the potion and Hannah drank it, making a face when she finished. "Will it work?"

"It has before."

Hannah and the nurse both stared at him and Doc's face reddened. He told Hazel to administer the drink twice more and then keep Hannah comfortable. Since a hospital had been built up on Tilden, they wouldn't be disturbed. Before he left, he made certain the chamber pot was ready.

Hannah lost her baby easily and two nights later, so did Annika.

Like all black markets, word was spread from mouth to mouth, and Doc became very popular with young women, most, but not all of them, single.

What he was doing didn't bother Doc; Nurse Hazel disposed of the blood, placenta, and the tiny human that came with it. Doc examined the young woman the next day and took whatever money she could afford.

Who knows how long Doc would have gone on? Abortion was illegal and punishable by a lengthy prison sentence, and there were rumors making the rounds about Doc's patients and their various abdominal illnesses. Still, no one had made a move to stop Doc, even those adamantly opposed to ending unborn life.

One night someone on Doc's floor was playing the Columbia recording "When My Baby Smiles at Me" by Ted Lewis and His Band. Doc was just about to turn in when he heard a knock. Expecting a young lady, he went to the door. Instead, it was the lawyer who had run with Doc's crowd in the old days.

After the usual pleasantries and the offer of a seat, the two men got down to business. The lawyer's daughter had gone off to college in Chicago and became a liberated woman: she bobbed her hair; wore amazingly short skirts; drank like a camel; and slept around, well, not "slept" exactly; but worse, she had gotten pregnant. And worse yet—the father was a Negro.

The lawyer said, "I'll not be the grandfather of a black bastard! I'd castrate the son of a bitch, but Nona says she doesn't know who it is; it could any of three, and I can't be neutering the entire male population of South Chicago, so I'll just get rid of the evidence. Or at least I want you to."

Since the men were friends, Doc agreed.

The next night Nona and her father appeared. When she took off her wrap, Doc was shocked: she was about seven-months pregnant. She was also adamant that she would have the baby. When her resolution ended in a gush of tears, Doc asked his friend to come with him to the examining room.

When Doc told him it was impossible for him to end the pregnancy with the concoction he had been using, not when someone was as far along as Nona was, the lawyer said, "Then operate."

"I can't...I won't." Doc's voice was shaking.

Over the next ten minutes Doc's mind was changed. His friend told him he knew Doc had been drunk when he operated on the appendicitis case so many years ago, and he would see that Doc was charged with murder if he didn't take care of Nona. Doc squirmed and begged, but he finally agreed, tears rolling down his cheeks.

Tears rolled down Nona's cheeks when she found out the abortion would take place. She made a break for the door and let loose a scream before her father clamped his hand over her mouth. Doc gave her a hypo and she settled into a dope-induced stupor.

Nurse Hazel was called and told to bring another nurse because Doc figured they'd have to hold Nona down, at least part of the time. Hazel recruited Ann Welch, fresh out of nursing school, but very strong. Hazel had heard nothing but praise for Ann's work at the hospital.

Nona was kept in a bed in the examining room until the next day when her cervix was dilated and held open. Doc kept her under morphine sedation.

When her water broke two days later, it was time. Nurse Ann was called in. Nona's father showed up in order to take her home that night. Her mother had passed away from consumption a decade before.

The nurses struggled to get dope-injected Nona into the operating room; she knew what was happening and hated it. She had been stripped and forced into a white gown. Placed on the table, she was strapped down and her legs were forced apart. They were also strapped.

Doc hesitated, but just for a moment: he hated the idea of open court and was petrified by a term in the state pen.

He picked up a spreader, inserted it, and opened the vagina, then dilated the cervix even more. Nurse Ann's face blanched: she thought it was a simple appendectomy she would be assisting at.

Doc took a long, stainless steel tool from a tray and inserted it. The metal was cold and Nona felt it. Doc pushed the shaft deep into the uterus and killed the baby. He suctioned out brain material and began the work of the forceps.

Over the next half hour the baby was pulled from the womb in pieces which were placed in a metal container, along with the placenta. A curette was used to scrape the sides of the uterus so no pieces were left inside. Even though she had been drugged, Nona struggled against her bonds in pain.

Finally, Doc was finished. Nurse Ann wiped his forehead for the final time.

Nona was taken to the examining room to recover. Nurse Ann was assigned to watch for bleeding. Nurse Hazel took the contents of the metal container and arranged them beside the sink into the shape of a baby. She called Doc over. "It's all here."

When he looked, he was surprised that the baby whose father was supposed to be a Negro had fairly white skin.

Nurse Hazel went to get a bag for the parts, leaving Doc alone with the jigsaw puzzle-baby. When Doc looked closer, he became aware of the fingernails. They were like perfect little pearls on the ends of perfect little fingers. Doc began to cry. He headed down the flight of stairs and went to his room where Nona's father waited. He saw the tears. "Doc, is everything all right?"

"She's resting. You'd better be with her." Doc didn't want the father around anymore. When he left, Doc locked the door. He took out the hypodermic and gave himself a shot of morphine, then lay on his bed and dreamed of tiny fingernails.

When Nurse Hazel felt that Nona was ready, she dismissed Nurse Ann and helped Nona get dressed. The lawyer went down to Doc's room and knocked at the door. "Doc, how much do I owe you?" No answer. "Doc, how much?" No answer. "I'll leave it under the door. If it's not enough, let me know." No answer. A hundred dollars was shoved under the door.

After helping Nona down the stairs and out to her father's Cadillac parked behind the hotel, Nurse Hazel cleaned up the mess and walked down Dakota Street to her house near the river. She was carrying a bag.

Nona lived with her father for a year and never said a kind word to him the entire time. In fact, most of the time, she had nothing to say to him at all. Finally, he couldn't take it anymore and said she could go back to college. When she boarded the train at the GN depot, the father and daughter did not embrace. He tried to tell her how much he loved her, but failed. All she said was "Goodbye." She never returned to Menninger.

That time she went to school at the University of Minnesota and majored in dramatic arts. Her father came to her graduation, but it was a cold reunion. The only reason she let him know the date was so he'd continue to send her monthly check to her new address which would be some place in Los Angeles. She had the acting bug.

At first, she got into a few crowd scenes and background roles in silent pictures, but when the talkies came in, her voice earned her some minor parts and three featured roles in B-Westerns under the name "Belle Bowman." She had dyed her light brown hair jet black, so it would make her more striking on the screen, and it worked, but it also made her appearance so much different that movie-goers in Menninger never recognized her. Then she decided to dye her hair white-blonde, but her timing was bad. Another white-blonde actress, Jean Harlow, hit it big with *The Public Enemy* and *Platinum Blonde*, and that effectively finished Nona's career.

Unfortunately, all her movies were shot on nitrate film base which deteriorated over the decades into goo and then dust, so that none of them could be salvaged when Hollywood and the Film World got around to saving their legacy. Nona would never be able to sit with her grandchildren and watch any of her old films on TV.

She did marry a movie producer who worked on the lot of Columbia Pictures and was one of a handful of people that got along with Columbia boss Harry Cohn. The couple had two sons who were adored by both parents, but especially by Nona. After five years of marriage, her husband grew tired of her lack of sexual drive and began taking a series of starlets as his mistresses. Nona didn't care; she had her boys and after they got married, she had her grandchildren.

Nona's father in North Dakota never saw them. Once she was married, Nona and her husband moved, and she didn't give her father the new address. She didn't need his money anymore.

Her father collapsed and died of a heart attack as he was leaving a café across from the Oleson House. No one knew how to reach his daughter, so she wasn't at the graveside when he was lowered to rest beside his wife. He left his estate to Nona and to the St. John's Orphanage in Fargo. After a fruitless search for Nona, the orphanage received the entire estate.

Nurse Ann couldn't work for several days after what she had witnessed. Then a month later she quit her job and went home to her parents. She even went back to her old religion which she had given up as being archaic. Eventually, she took vows and became a member of the Sisters of St. Francis of the Immaculate Heart of Mary, an order that had just started a convent in Kelly, North Dakota. She dedicated her life to teaching young students and serving those in need.

Nurse Hazel didn't work as a nurse once Doc retired; the other doctors didn't like her and she didn't like them. Nurse Hazel was a biological rarity: she was a human freemartin. In the womb with her twin brother, some of his male material went into her system via the placentas. There was no irreversible effect on her brother, with the exception of slightly smaller testicles, but Hazel was born with ovaries that would never function.

While her teenage girlfriends were lamenting, but secretly celebrating, the onset of menstruation and budding breasts, Hazel had to lie to keep up with them. Later when marriages and children enveloped her friends, she pulled away. She was not an attractive woman and when her voice deepened and her facial hair became too obvious, she isolated herself from the world of friends, even of acquaintances, and began shaving her face. She finished her nurse's training at the top of her class, but she was the only one without a friend to share the happiness of the moment. Her parents and twin brother had all perished in a house fire while he was home from college. When she appeared for the funeral, she could hear people commenting on her appearance. Was she really a woman?

She hated the world, so she moved out of Ohio and ended up in Menninger. People still talked, but Doc gave her a job as his nurse, and she never forgot. In some ways, but obviously not all, he became like a husband, and they developed a mutual support system.

She couldn't get Doc off the dope, no matter how she tried, and her visits to the Oleson became fewer and fewer. Sometimes he didn't even know her.

Although Menninger had a water and sewer system that eventually encompassed the entire town, Hazel had kept the wooden single-hole outhouse that had come with the place. Her neighbors thought she did it to spite them, but the real reason was she had dumped the remnants of Doc's abortions down the hole.

Also, sometimes she liked to use the facility and just sit and think.

One winter her pipes froze up after a snowstorm, so she made her way through the drifts, shoveled open the door, and got ready to do her business. She didn't want to stay too long because it was ten below zero.

One of her neighbors noticed that there had been no activity at Hazel's house for two days, so she sent her husband over to investigate. Maybe the poor thing had fallen; after all she must be seventy years old.

After not finding anyone in the big house, the man checked the little house out back. Hazel was frozen solid, a victim of a stroke and the Dakota winter.

Nineteen people attended her funeral in the Methodist Church; only Doc cried.

It couldn't really be said that Doc Blanchard lived after his last abortion. He floated along in a morphine fog.

He found the money under the door and gave it all to Hiram, the town drunk, who had it all spent in two days after buying blind pig liquor for himself and his alky friends and a new collar for his dog, a huge, but gentle, black Lab named Jack Johnson.

After that, it was morphine dreams because his regular dreams were plagued by tiny pearl fingernails on tiny fingers.

The years slipped by; most of the time Doc didn't even know what year it was. His dark hair bushed out and turned into a shock of white. He would have one meal a day in the Oleson dining room, usually the soup of the day and a cold sandwich. Then his gaunt figure would slowly climb the stairs. His friends dropped away, or like Hazel, died.

Even worse, the little pearls began to invade his drug-induced dreams; then when he woke up, stone-cold and drug-free, he started to see little hands, little fingers, beckoning him.

A letter informed him that his parents had died within a week of each other, and his brother and sister were stopping the family's financial support. Doc became a charity case, supported by the county which paid his room and board in the Oleson. Luckily, he had hoarded enough morphine to last a lifetime. Or at least the lifetime of a junky.

The man who used to have such a sense of humor that guests would sit near his table just to hear what observations or jokes he would make, stopped laughing, stopped smiling. Eric and Lena remarked about how much they missed Doc's smile.

Eric and Lena had to close off the fourth floor when their customer base began dwindling. Then they closed most of the rooms on the third floor, except for Doc's and two by the stairs. The dining room was next.

After Doc died, the third floor was closed and his room remained exactly as it had been the day he passed away on the roof.

Maybe he felt Death approaching; maybe he just wanted some sunlight and fresh air; maybe it was just a coincidence that it was the anniversary of the day he had aborted Nona. Anyway, he left his room and walked up the stairs, then climbed a ladder to gain access to the roof. When he opened the trap door, he scared away a crow.

Not too much later the crow returned, to be joined by another. Eventually, two dozen crows were on the roof, raising such a racket that Eric had to call the chief of police to check on the situation. The chief arrived with another officer and two volunteer firemen.

Two of the old men standing in the room littered with red containers had been on the roof so many years before. They were telling a group of students and anyone else who cared to listen what they had seen.

"Doc was on his back. The crows had pecked out his eyes." Several students, most of them girls, made sounds of revulsion.

The other man spoke. "And the birds had been at his cheeks and lips. His teeth showed, so it looked like he had a smile on his face...a gaunt smile...the first one in years."

HORSE SCREAMS

—— 🌀 ——

I am a hypocrite.

In the summer of 1923, my two friends Merle and Pearl Potman, their cousin Axel, and I rode trains to San Francisco, where my brother Josh and his family lived. Josh was a big believer in the natural rights of life and property, and as he talked to me, I became a believer, too. After I got home, I read about natural rights theory and became even more of a believer.

My Dad, known as Boss, wasn't really that upset that I had taken off for the Coast without telling anyone, but he decided to give me a job that would keep me close to home. He spoke to me at supper. He had taken a flyer on raising some beef cattle on a pasture north of the Jacques River, and it would be my job to check on them every day to see that none of them had gotten out or were sick or hurt and that they had plenty of water.

"Do you think you can handle it?"

I had just picked up my glass of milk. "Sure, I'd like it." I took a big drink. I like milk, so pure and white. Ours was delivered by the milkman in glass bottles. We'd leave an empty bottle or two on the front porch the night before, and when we went out the next morning, there was the milk, pasteurized and homogenized at the Blue Ribbon Creamery. In the cold months if we didn't get out there early enough, the milk would be frozen and the caps would be an inch or so above the bottle on a little column of milky ice. I finished my milk and used a napkin. Milk was perfect.

I could have ridden my Hawthorne De Luxe bicycle, but sometimes the Herefords were on the far side of the pasture, and the ground was pretty lumpy, so I borrowed Lawrence Larson's horse, "Jack." The Larsons lived next door, and their barn was on the alley, so I'd put a bridle on Jack and ride bareback to Salem Street, head north to Mill Avenue, west to Glen Haven, north again, cross the bridge over the Jacques, and continue the two miles to the pasture.

After riding smoky trains and being in a big city on the trip to the Coast, I enjoyed the smell of the country and even of Jack. I liked the way the reins felt in my hands and the movement of Jack's muscles against my knees. Even after school took up, I looked forward to my job—at least it kept my mind on something until hunting season began.

One afternoon I had just cleared the bridge when I heard yelling and cursing and some high-pitched horse-noise coming from Charles Simon's barn.

Simon wasn't his real name. His folks had come from Romania with a surname no one could spell, so his father changed it to "Simon." He also changed Charles's Christian name from "Cezar."

The family settled on a hard-scrabble farm northwest of Menninger, but Mrs. Simon missed the Old Country. She'd lasted a couple years and died. She was buried in a "No Stone" grave in Eternal Rest Cemetery. Some people said her death was the reason Simon was so mean. Others claimed he was the reason for her death, what with his terrible temper even as a boy. Whichever way you believed, he was one mean SOB.

Eventually, his father lost the farm, moved into town, and died.

Simon got a loan from the bank, engineered by Boss, and bought ten acres just north of the river where he raised vegetables and corn to sell. He had a small house and a somewhat larger barn. He had two horses— Buck and Bright—that looked like twins. They were sorrels, with four white stockings and a white flash down their noses. He inherited them when he bought the property, but as the years passed, they lost a lot of sheen from their coats and a lot of their spirit. Even so, he continued to use them for plowing and some minor draying.

Boss would hire him to plow up our garden plot. It wasn't that big, but Boss wanted to help out an immigrant, or at least an immigrant's son.

I liked to watch the plow slice into the soil and listen to Simon yelling commands to his team, but it was sad to see how the horses had been reduced from a great matched pair to a couple of thin working drudges in just five years.

From the barn I heard, "Voi Devils! I…kill…you, you…bastards! Nemernici! You sons of bitches!" A whip-sound punctuated his words.

"I want you to stop whipping your horses!"

He glared at me until recognition flashed across his face. "You are Boss's son?"

"Yes."

"A fine man." He put down the whip. In their stalls both Buck and Bright looked back over their shoulders.

"Yes, but I don't want you to whip your horses."

"Sometimes is necessary. They must obey."

"Yes, but sometimes there are better ways."

"Sometimes not." The glare was coming back.

"How much do you want for them?"

"You want to buy?"

"Yes, how much?"

"If I sell, I cannot plow or pull; I cannot make money."

I walked over to the stalls. The skin was not broken on either horse; there was no bleeding. There were a lot of people in town who knew Simon was mistreating his horses, but unless the whip marks showed or they were scarred, no one would do anything.

"So you won't sell?"

"No."

We were at an impasse. "All right, but please don't beat them." The glare came back, but no words. I left.

I thought maybe my sympathy for the horses would carry the day, that Simon would stop abusing his animals, but a week later I heard the high-pitched horse-screams and the cursing again. I turned into the yard, dismounted, and ran inside the barn.

It was the same old scene: Simon laying on the leather and the curses, while Buck and Bright attempted to dodge the whip by smashing into the sides of their stalls. The worst thing, though, wasn't the flailing whip; it was their screams.

I grabbed Simon by the shoulders, spun him around, and gave him a right to the jaw. He went down. I picked up the whip and retreated toward the door. We were about the same size, so I expected an attack. He got up and thought about it, but apparently decided on another course of action. I went out into the sunlight. I faced Jack's tail, grabbed a handful of mane, hopped onto my left leg, and vaulted onto his back, twisting so my right leg slid down his far side. I rode out to the cows, my body hot with anger.

On my way back home, I stopped Jack on the bridge and hurled the whip as far as I could into the Jacques.

The next day a knock on our front door informed our family that I was being sued for assault and battery. After confirming that I had knocked Simon down, Boss called Grandpa Bear, and they went down to talk with Simon.

I don't know what they said, but when they got back, the charges had been dropped; however, Boss told me I couldn't go near Simon again, no matter the circumstances.

At first, that was easy: riding Jack out to work and back, feeling his muscles as we headed up the hill to home, not hearing anything but birds and the rattle of stones kicked by Jack's hooves. A couple weeks later, however, I heard the shrill screams from the barn again. What was Simon using? Did he have an extra whip? Was it a piece of wood? A lathe? Or worse, a 2x4? Going up the hill was a depressing exercise in uncertainty while I felt Jack's strong back and thought of the sore backs of Buck and Bright. What should I do?

Sometimes it's better to talk things over with your friends than to make an ultimate decision by yourself, so I went over to Merle and Pearl Potman's place. The twins were my best friends and I needed their advice on how to handle Simon.

We sat in their backyard by the alley, swigging some lemonade their mother brought out, and hatched a plan.

We had to wait a week for a new moon, then we dressed in black, met at the bridge, crossed over, and belly-crawled our way to the barn. Simon used to have a dog, a huge spotted beast that kept everyone off his property, but one day Simon showed up in town with a large rag wrapped around his hand. The dog was never seen again. That was our good fortune.

Buck and Bright were quiet as we bridled-up, and the twins led them out of the barn and downriver on the north bank. We kept going, but not as far as where the three Sullivan sisters drowned in 1897. We stripped off our boots and clothes, bundled them, and mounted—Merle on Buck; Pearl and me on Bright. We swam the horses across the river. The water level was down, so the horses were able to walk some of the way.

Mid-September may still be summer on the calendar, but at night, it's autumn. We sat on some big rocks, waiting to dry. The rocks were still warm from the day, at least warmer than the air. No one said much, except Pearl mentioned once again his desire to go into radio broadcasting and that a clear night was the best time for radio. Buck and Bright munched on some grass as if they hadn't gotten enough to eat for awhile.

The Summer Triangle of Deneb, bright blue-white Vega, and Altair was no longer overhead, so summer was coming to an end. I still enjoyed looking at them and at the white dotty film of the Milky Way. I hoped that if I ever had a son, he would enjoy the stars as much as I did.

Finally, we were dry enough and got dressed. Now came the tricky part of our plan.

We were in Winslow's pasture, and even though the chances were slim, we waited until we were certain no one was about. Pearl moved ahead as a scout, Merle took Buck, and I led Bright. The lights of the town showed to the west.

We'd move a few dozen yards and wait for Pearl to report, then move again. We opened the gate and moved through. Pearl shut it and went scouting again.

We moved into the Addition prompted when the Great Northern built through town a decade before. Houses ran along the shoulder of the hill, and a few people had actually built down in the valley toward the river, but the dwellings were scattered, so we stayed away from the hill.

We crossed Sixth Street East easily—there were no houses to our right—but Fifth Street was a problem. The yards of the houses on the hill ran down and ended at the alley. Plus, there were several houses to our right.

Pearl went down the alley and came back. "All clear." We moved out. Suddenly there was a whinny from a barn on the right. Both Buck and Bright gave out a "chough," so we hurried them along before they got louder.

At Fourth Street Pearl went up the hill. He was gone a long time. When he came back, he explained that a couple, out for stroll, had stopped for some kissing and then hurried on their way. No one else was in sight.

We moved up the hill, crossed Stimson Avenue, and turned in our alley. Another horse called from the first barn, and we tugged on the bridles and got moving until we reached Larsons' barn. Pearl pulled the door open, we went in, and he shut it.

Jack was a friendly horse and nuzzled Buck and Bright as we moved past him.

As part of my job, I had to feed and water Jack and muck out the barn, so extra rations for Buck and Bright weren't a problem. The problem was I had to get up at 6:30.

After our long night and my early morning, school was tough. I almost fell asleep in Assembly; the rift between a girl I liked, Emily Livingstone, and me was growing; and my troubles with Physics continued.

When I rode past Simon's place after school, he came charging out of the ditch, yelling that I had stolen his horses. "I kill you, son of a bitch! Horse thief!" He laid a knotted rein across my back; I could sympathize with Buck and Bright. I kneed Jack into flight and Simon's curses followed us north.

On the way back I urged Jack into a gallop, and we were on the bridge before Simon could react.

I wasn't very worried about the discovery of the two horses because the Larsons' didn't pay much attention to Jack after I took over his care, just a Sunday afternoon drive around the town or a short tour of the countryside.

I did get worried at supper when Boss said that someone had stolen Simon's team. He looked at me. "Lige, do you know anything about it?"

I was stuck because I couldn't lie to Boss over something so serious, but then he saved me. "I mean…well…in plain English…did you steal those horses?"

I looked squarely at him. "No, I did not take those horses from Simon's barn."

"On your honor?"

"Yes."

"That's good enough for me. I'll tell Simon when he talks to me again tomorrow."

I could breathe once more, but I did feel a little guilty. Someday I'd tell Boss the whole story.

About midnight I sneaked out my window again, crossed the porch roof, and shinnied down the big box elder to the ground. My dog Ted was in his usual nighttime place, the garage to the east of the house, so I walked around the west side down to the alley and over to the Larsons' barn.

Merle and Pearl were already at work. They had purchased some cans of boot polish—some tan and some oxblood—and by mixing them the resulting color blended reasonably well with the color of Buck and Bright. I joined them in smearing it on their white forehead patch and white stockings. The flashlight showed it wasn't a perfect match, but it only had to last until the afternoon.

We put the bridles on and headed down the alley, Pearl acting again as our scout. We turned on Salem and headed south. We went past the three-story school on the left and the Baptist and Congo churches on our right. Pearl kept half a block ahead, but never gave the danger signal, flashing an "X" with the light. At Dunnell Merle and I mounted—just two boys out for a late-night ride.

We crossed the GN tracks and turned west on Gorringe. Our town had three stockyards; the two on the GN—one a mile west of town and one across from the depot—handled mostly cattle, pigs, and sheep; the one on the NP at the end of Gorringe shipped mostly horses.

The horse trade wasn't like it had been during the Great War when all the stockyards were shipping horses faster than they could be rounded up. With the end of the war, only a Montana cowboy, Joe King, dealt in horse flesh. He'd arrive in mid-summer and scour the farms and ranches for horses, then a couple times in August and September, he'd load horses onto cars from the stockyards at Lakeside, Divide, and Menninger, and they'd go to auction in the Twin Cities. And it wasn't to glue factories, either. Farmers in Minnesota, Iowa, and Illinois would put in their bids, just the reverse of the 1880s and 1890s when those states had supplied the northern plains with horses.

There were about twenty animals in the corral, and they started milling when we opened the gate and Buck and Bright went in. Pearl got busy looking for two similar geldings, while Merle and I took off the bridles. I patted and smoothed Buck and Bright. Merle wasn't that attached to them and didn't have to say goodbye. Joe King didn't want any bronchos, so it was easy to approach the two geldings Pearl found and bridle up.

We mounted, Pearl opened the gate, and we went out. Pearl shut the gate, handed the flashlight to Merle, and headed for home.

Merle and I and our new mounts headed to South Avenue and went west across the NP tracks. The trees of the Pepple Grove shielded us from the town.

I figured Joe King would count his animals and when the number was correct, not have any reason to question the authenticity of any of them. Buck and Bright would be loaded with the rest and start a new life, a life ten times better, maybe a hundred times better, than the one they were leaving.

It bothered me that I was breaking one of my rules: the sanctity of private property. As we rode the horses, the night sky sparked above us. The little star puzzles known as constellations winked their cold lights: the Big and Little Dippers off to the north, Cassiopeia and Hercules overhead, Aquarius and Aquila to the south, and many others I couldn't pick out.

Each star was a separate creation, just as a person's mind and body were separate from all other minds and bodies.

My mind existed: "Cogito ergo sum" as Descartes wrote; "I think, therefore I am." Every time you thought you reaffirmed your mind's existence. Other minds and bodies existed, also. If I told Merle that Cecilia Livingstone was an ugly pig, I could expect a punch in the nose and it would hurt. My mind told my vocal cords what to say, and Merle's mind and body, separate from mine, reacted.

Leaving aside the insane and the feebleminded, a person's mind, separate from all others, was owned and controlled by that person. If that were not the case, then some other mind would have the right to control yours. Some people such as Nietzsche tried to argue that was true, but I didn't believe they had proven their point: What in the realm of creation gave one mind the power to control another? Just saying it, didn't make it so.

Many people in the past had controlled the bodies of others through slavery and force, but if each mind were separate and equal, then bodies, in a moral sense, were, too. People owned and controlled their own bodies. If that were not so, then someone else could own and control them. To me it was a lot easier to defend the idea that all people were separate beings and morally equal to all other people than it would be to argue that force and violence or some form of moral superiority gave the "superior" people the power to "own" others.

If a person owned and controlled his or her own mind and body, by extension that person could use that mind and body to transform natural resources mixed with their own abilities into ownable things, including services.

The question then became who owned the goods and services the free individual produced? Did they belong to the individual producer or did someone else own and/or control them?

It followed logically that a good or service produced by a free individual belonged to that individual. Those who believed the good or service became the property of the State, the community, society, the slave owners, etc., had the burden of proof on their side. I believed in the concept of private property, whether it was created, bought, inherited, or bartered for.

But that led to my dilemma. Simon was a free individual. He had purchased Buck and Bright, along with the land and buildings, and, unless animals had rights to their own lives and liberty, he could do with them as he chose.

As far as I knew, no animals had a concept of self-awareness which took them beyond the instinct level for self-preservation. No animal could conceive of natural rights, much less communicate such a concept.

When I looked into the eyes of Buck and Bright or my dog Ted, I could see living beings, but they were not beings that were capable of formulating and defending concepts and therefore could not be said to have natural rights to life and property, which they could clearly not comprehend.

And yet I couldn't stand to see them beaten into screams, so I rode on to the west.

We rode over a rise and turned south. The several families that lived on the surrounding land contended with rocks, creeks, ponds, a small lake, sloughs, marshes, rolling topography, and one long gully eroding out of the gravelly soil. It wasn't the best land for farming, but cattle and sheep could make it. Horses, too, and we knew there were several large horse herds in the pastures.

Merle opened a gate and we went through into a pasture. Once we'd seen a little claybank mare frisking in that pasture and wished she belonged to us. I thought maybe she was still there and Buck and Bright might meet her; then I thought of their condition and figured they wouldn't care one way or the other. We took off the bridles and spanked the horses on their rumps. Away they went, hopefully to blend in with a herd for at least a couple weeks. We closed the gate, tossed the bridles into a steep-sided ditch, and headed for town. The bridles were Simon's private property, and I should have returned them, but I figured "in for a penny, in for a pound."

Two hours' sleep added to a previous sleep-shortened night, and I couldn't keep my eyes open in English class—"Mr. Cockburn, Detention!"

I was late getting out to the Herefords. There was no activity at Simon's place, but Boss said he had been in town raising "Holy Heck." If

Ma hadn't been in the room, he would have used a different term. After supper I went down to the NP stockyards; they were empty.

Saturday was round-up day. Johnny Strong, Pete Martin, Boss, and I drove the Herefords from their pasture, up the Glen Haven hill, and down Lamborn and Chicago to the GN stockyards. Boss was on one of Johnny's horses, and I was on Jack.

Even before the War very few men rode into town on horseback; they came in on farm wagons or in buggies. After the war a lot of them switched over to automobiles, so being astride horses made us really stand out. I thought we looked just like some old-time cowpunchers pushing a herd into Dodge City, and since Chicago was our main street, I got plenty of admiring looks from the girls.

We penned the cattle, school days crawled along, and things were settling down. By things I mean Simon and his rantings and my conscience. Then about a week later Boss brought up Simon at the supper table by telling Ma and me that he had left town. The reason was that he had tried to buy a team to replace Buck and Bright, but that no one would sell him any horses because they knew he would only mistreat them. That made me feel good, but I wondered where the men had been when Buck and Bright were being beaten.

"We bought him out." Boss looked at me. The "we" meant the bank of which Boss was the president. "He packed up and left on the south-bound. Good riddance. He had no principles, no real values. We don't need men like that in our town. I guess we should have forced him out a long time ago, but better late than never."

Ma said, "I never did like that man. We ladies knew what he was doing and wondered why you men didn't stop it."

"I guess we finally found our principles. Any man who beats his animals doesn't deserve to live in civilized society, maybe any society. A man must live up to his principles, right, Lige?"

"Yes, Boss." I hid my hypocrisy behind a big drink of milk.

MAGGIE: A GIRL

M argarete "Maggie" Vogler was sure of two things: she loved geography and Manfred Friedrich Vogler was not her father.

He was married to Maggie's mother Hedy (no one called her by her real name, Hedwig), but Maggie was certain he was really a stepfather. No real father would treat her the way he did. Many times sent to bed without supper, slapped, spanked, whipped with his belt or razor strop, just thinking about them made Maggie cringe. Even though she would say "father" or "my father" when she talked to him or to other people, in her mind she always referred to him as "M.F."

She nestled down in the covers and opened her book, her only book. It was old; the covering on the spine was worn through; a couple pages had rips; but it was hers, and she loved it. The title was *Harper's Introductory Geography* and the copyright date was 1877. The Western Hemisphere appeared in a circle on the front cover, and the Eastern Hemisphere was in a circle on the back cover. The continents and oceans were named. On the inside of the cover were the words "Donated to the Menninger Public School by Miss Anna Dickson, Sept. 13, 1894."

Maggie was only twelve years old, but she had already been in ten states, although she didn't remember them all. Her mother had told her about her birth in Missouri, how cute she was, and how she learned to walk. There was a trip through Illinois to see her grandparents in Wisconsin, where they lived for awhile. Then a move to Iowa, but none of her mother's stories like the one where Maggie got lost in a cornfield and a collie found her triggered any memories. She did have vague recollections of a hot summer in Topeka, Kansas, and having ice put around her to keep her cool. Maggie had strong memories of the other states: Nebraska, where they lived in her uncle and aunt's house; Minnesota; Montana; South Dakota; and North Dakota. Sometimes not good memories.

Manfred had been in the Army, where he was a cook. However, he'd never gone overseas; he spent his time at both Camp Upton and Camp Mills on Long Island, preparing food for thousands of soldiers about to embark for Europe.

Manfred's younger brother Alfred was one of those "dough boys," but he never returned. He was killed on the banks of the Marne River, helping to stop a German advance. His death was devastating to the entire family, but Manfred took it the worst. He began drinking so badly that he was given a dishonorable discharge after attacking an officer who questioned whether he was sober or not.

When he finally arrived in Omaha, Maggie rushed to give her Papa (she still called him that then) a big hug. He brushed her off and walked unsteadily across the depot platform to collapse in the front seat of his brother-in-law's automobile. He began to snore heavily on the drive home.

Papa took a job as a cook in the Prague Hotel restaurant, but quit two weeks later because he couldn't stand listening to all the babble by the "Bohunks." He cooked at the Flatiron Hotel restaurant for a couple months, but his drinking got him fired. He offered to work cheap at Father Flanagan's Home for Boys, but the young Irish priest would have none of him after he checked into his background.

Maggie started the first grade in Omaha. Luckily, the school was only six blocks away because she had to walk. Even better, her cousin, Linda Kaye, was in the same class, so they could walk together. Most of the time she liked being with Linda Kaye, but not when she talked about Papa drinking poison. That was silly because he would be dead, but Linda Kaye swore she heard her Mommy and Daddy say just that.

Maggie's mother told her how Papa would sometimes bring home little treats from the cooking jobs he'd had before the Army. Maggie couldn't remember them, but she felt good that Papa would remember her with a cookie or a little piece of cake, even if they were day-old. In Omaha she kept waiting for Papa to bring something good home to her and her mother, but he never did. Then one evening when she was helping set the table, she dropped a cup and it broke on the linoleum. A quick slash of Papa's hand and her cheek crimsoned. She was sent to bed with no supper. Under the covers her heart hurt longer than her cheek. Her heart hurt even worse when she could hear Papa and Mama fighting. Sometimes her aunt and uncle would also join in, always against Papa.

When she got up the next morning, Papa was just leaving. She ran to him and said, "Papa, I'm sorry…about the cup."

He glared down at her. "You should be." He slammed the door.

By that time Hedy's sister Aunt Bruna was hinting maybe the Voglers should leave. After a verbal altercation between an angry Uncle Jerry and a drunk Manfred, the sisters said goodbye. The next stop was Lincoln, where Maggie was enrolled in a school only four blocks away.

Manfred hooked a job with the Chicago, Burlington & Quincy Railroad as a line cook specializing in bread and pastries. He'd board the "Q" in Lincoln and ride it to Denver and back.

In Lincoln, Maggie was glad he was away on the train so much of the time.

Just as the school year was ending, some men came to the front door dragging Papa along. They left him on the living room floor. One of the men told Hedy that he'd come to work drunk, and after he was fired, he'd gone on a "toot" which left him unconscious.

Hedy clutched her stomach; she was pregnant. She couldn't lift Manfred, so she covered him with a blanket, and he slept away his stupor, drooling on the linoleum. They would have to move.

Their next stop was Chaska, Minnesota, where Manfred got a job as a cook at a lunch counter near the M.A. Gedney Pickling Company. He cut down on his drinking, which Maggie liked, but he came home smelling of vinegar and sauerkraut. She didn't like sauerkraut.

She did like her new little brother Johan Alfred, who soon became "John." She was thrilled the first time she was allowed to hold him and he smiled at her, or at least she thought it was a smile.

That fall Manfred got a new job: cooking at the four-story Minnesota Sugar Company plant. Some of the seasonal workers lived in company-owned boarding houses. Things seemed to be going well. Also that fall Maggie started the second grade. At first, she was sad because there was no Linda Kaye to walk and talk with, but then she made friends with two girls: Clara, who left when the seasonal workers at the beet plant were let go, and Constance, or "Connie," as she wanted to be called.

Only twice during the year did Manfred come home drunk, and both times Maggie ended up being swatted and sent to bed with no supper for breaking his invisible rules. When she told Connie about it, Connie said her Daddy was the same way. The girls vowed that when they got married, their husbands would never drink or hit. To seal the vow, they linked their pinky fingers and spit, the way the boys did.

Connie and Maggie were best friends in the third grade, but then came the anniversary of the death of Private Alfred Vogler, and Manfred didn't show up for work. He was blind drunk at a blind pig halfway to Shakopee. No one knew how he got there or how he got home. All his boss knew was that he was no longer needed.

Maggie had less than a week to say goodbye to Connie. They spent their recess time off by the chain-link fence talking and most of the time ended up crying. They said they would write to each other, but, of course, they never did: neither one was very good at writing and once Maggie left, both girls discovered they didn't know the other one's address.

Maggie finished the third grade in Great Falls, Montana. Manfred started a job as a short-order cook in a beanery downtown, but with the Anaconda Copper Mining Company, the Great Northern Railway, the Black Eagle Dam for power, and moneyed businessmen, Great Falls was booming, and good cooks were at a premium. Soon he was cooking in a café which catered to the workers at the copper smelter.

The Voglers had never owned an automobile, so it was a treat whenever Maggie got to ride in one. On a Sunday afternoon in May, Manfred's friend Louis and his girlfriend Belle came around in a large black car and took the Voglers for a drive. As Maggie looked at the traffic, the trains, and all the buildings, she suddenly noticed a large smokestack set up on a hill. Smoke was surging out and went wafting away in the wind.

"That's where I work," Louis said. "That's the smelter."

Smelter. That was a funny word. Maggie began to giggle. Manfred, who was riding with Belle and Louis in the front seat, turned around and shot a black glare at Maggie. Her mother pulled her close and whispered, "Shhh." Baby John just stared.

Maggie enjoyed the sights and sounds, if not the smells, of Great Falls, but eventually they headed for home. As they were driving, Louis pulled out a long cigar, bit off and spit out an end, and had Belle light it for him. He took a big drag and the smoke jetted out and was caught by the breeze. He looked just like the big smoke stack. Maggie started to laugh.

Once again she got the black stare.

When she said goodbye to Louis and Belle, she thanked them for the ride and made a little curtsey, the way she'd been taught. Belle laughed and said, "That's so cute." Maggie felt good walking into her house. Then Manfred came in.

"Maggie, come here."

Maggie expected to be praised for her good manners. Instead, she saw Papa was angry.

"I won't have you laughing at my friends."

Maggie tried to explain she wasn't laughing at Louis, but Manfred unbuckled and swished out his belt, grabbed her, and bent her over his knee. Hedy fled from the room with Baby John.

In bed without supper again, Maggie lay on her stomach and sobbed. She never thought of Manfred as Papa again.

In Great Falls Manfred picked up another vice: cheap cigars. The band on the cigar could picture a wolf, an Indian, a horse, it didn't matter as long as it wasn't over a nickel. Maggie began to hate the smell of cigars.

Fourth grade began in Great Falls, and she had two friends, Judy and Sheila. Judy's father was a baker, and she'd share cookies and cake with

Maggie and Sheila at lunchtime. Maggie was ashamed she didn't have anything to give in return. Sheila didn't have a father; Maggie envied her.

Manfred's reputation as a cook grew, and he was hired at the prestigious Rainbow Hotel on North 3rd Street. He was ashamed of the clothes he had to come to work in, so most of his first paychecks went into a new wardrobe for himself. Even though he looked elegant as he paraded out the door to go to work, Maggie didn't care.

Although he wasn't the head chef, Manfred felt tremendous pressure at the Rainbow. His legs would quiver and his heart would palpitate when he learned he would be helping prepare a meal for John D. Ryan of Anaconda Copper, Louis W. Hill of the Great Northern, or some other rich and powerful man.

After finding a favorite bootlegger, Manfred began taking the edge off his nerves with an occasional nip from the bottle he had hidden in the men's washroom. Soon, it became more than occasional and soon after that he was out of a job.

The family piled onto the "Oriental Limited" and rode the GN to St. Paul.

After being rejected as a cook by the "Q" for obvious reasons, Manfred caught on with the Milwaukee Road's "Pioneer Limited" which ran between the Twin Cities and Chicago.

Maggie was enrolled at St. Matthew's Catholic School as a charity case. It was the closest school to their home, located in a German immigrant community, and Hedy pleaded with the head administrator, tears in her eyes, to give her daughter a chance. If he had known that Manfred was an atheist and Hedy was a non-practicing Lutheran, he might not have been so compliant.

Maggie disliked the discipline of the nuns and the cold shoulders she got from the other students, but her reading and writing improved, and she discovered geography. In fact, it was the one subject she excelled in.

One day Sister Martha had everyone choose a country. The students were going to make maps. But not just any maps—they were going to be clay made out of flour and salt and water. And the students would make the clay. Everyone began talking at once. Even Alicia with the buck teeth who sat in the desk across from Maggie smiled her toothy smile;

Maggie couldn't help smiling back. Then it was quiet: Sister Martha was frowning. No one wanted her to stop the project before it had even gotten started.

Maggie enjoyed mixing the salt and flour and then adding the water. Sister Martha supervised her students: some mixtures needed more water, some more salt and flour if they were too watery. When Maggie's was just right, Sister Martha told her, "Just keep mushing and mixing with your hands." Maggie liked the feel of the clay-dough, but mixing it was awfully tiring.

The students had to work at the mixing for several days because only fifteen minutes were allotted to the project. Starting the mixing process the next day was always hard because the dough would stiffen overnight. Eventually, however, it was ready.

Sister Martha gave each student a piece of cardboard and showed them how to put down a layer of flour on it so the dough wouldn't stick and how to outline their country. Then she made a dough-map of North Dakota, sloping the dough up from the Red River Valley, pinching up the Turtle Mountains, grooving the major rivers, and jabbing little slits for the Badlands.

Her students were fascinated, and the next day when she unveiled North Dakota and about an inch of Canada, Montana, South Dakota, and Minnesota, with the rivers and lakes in blue, the Red River Valley in dark green, the Drift Prairies in light green, the dry western parts in brown, the Badlands in reddish-brown, and the Turtle Mountains in gray, the children were enthralled, especially Maggie.

The next day they all went to work, but it was Friday, so they had to put away their things unfinished. Maggie went home anticipating Monday so much she didn't even bother to care that M.F. came home drunk and snored all night on the ratty davenport. All Maggie thought about was "Italy," the country she'd chosen.

The next week was all Maggie's to enjoy. Italy's "boot" appeared on her cardboard. She pinched up the Apennines and the Alps, grooved out the Po, the Tiber, and the Arno, checked the atlas and added Sicily and Sardinia because those islands belonged to Italy, and put in special tiny pinches for Mt. Vesuvius and Mt. Etna.

Sister Martha walked around and checked on everyone's project, but never told anyone if she approved or not—the project was for a grade.

After a dough-map was ready, it was whisked away to the kitchen, where the cooks would bake it. When it was returned the next day, all hard and white, the student would paint in the details just as Sister had done. Then it was placed on the cardboard and put away under a couple old sheets until all the projects were finished.

On the day of the unveiling, Sister had a treat. The cooks had made something special: food from most of the countries on the map. The few in Africa were left out because no one knew how to make the foods mentioned in the geography books.

After everyone had finished eating and drinking, it was time for the maps to be passed back. Maggie squirmed in her seat. The anticipation was so great she thought her heart would burst. Sister placed Spain on Alicia's desk, and Alicia read the note Sister had written her and her letter grade.

Maggie saw that Alicia had included Portugal and part of France north of the Pyrenees, so she knew Alicia couldn't have gotten a very good grade: her country was Spain, not Portugal or France.

When Alicia leaned over behind Sister's back and said, "I got an A," Maggie couldn't understand such a grading system.

Finally, her map was placed in front of her. It was beautiful. She opened the note: C-. It couldn't be; it was a mistake. She read the note: "Maggie, you did an excellent job on your map and its colors, but did not put in Corsica, France, Switzerland, Austria, or the Dalmatian Coast. Always be thorough."

Alicia whispered, "What did you get?"

Maggie was too busy choking on her tears.

"I'll bet it was an A+; you're always so good at geography."

The dismissal bell rang. The children automatically stood beside their desks, and Sister led them in a "Hail Mary," then told them to leave their projects; they could pick them up the next day and show their parents.

The walk home was six blocks, six blocks of cold for Maggie and not just because of the February weather. Alicia was beside her for one block;

she wouldn't stop talking about her A. Maggie would not allow herself to cry; instead, she thought of ways she could approach Sister and explain why "Italy" to her meant just "Italy" and not its neighbors. Maybe Sister would let her fix her map with more dough and paint to fill in the missing parts. Even if it didn't change her grade, at least she'd be proud enough of her work to show Mama.

She began to feel better as she neared home, except for the toe of the stocking on her right foot that had a hole which Mama had darned. Her shoes were too small and the darn hurt her big toe.

Up ahead she saw Mama on what passed as a sidewalk. The Voglers didn't own a stick of furniture, but all their suitcases, carry-all's, and small trunks were beside her; it was as if she was guarding them.

"Oh, Maggie; I'm glad you're here. Watch over our things. Papa will be here soon." She rushed into the house.

Maggie looked around, wondering what was going on. She saw some of the neighbors staring at her from their front steps. Suddenly a car pulled up and M.F. jumped out. "V'ere's your mudder?" Maggie pointed. Manfred ran.

A minute later he came out, dragging Mama and Baby John. The driver and Manfred threw the luggage into the car, nearly covering Hedy and the two children, then hurled themselves into the front seat and away the driver sped.

"Mama, what's wrong?" Maggie whispered.

Mama whispered back, "Papa is in trouble with some bad men, but he went to a pawn shop with his good clothes and got enough money so we can get away....It will be all right; you'll see."

They drove to the St. Paul Union Depot, which impressed Maggie with its large stone columns. While the luggage was being taken inside, Manfred bought tickets. The driver refused the money Manfred offered, wished him luck, and was gone. Manfred lurked in the concourse and lobby, while the rest of the family sat in the main waiting room. On a sunny day the skylights would have been blinding with light, but in early spring they were dusky. Maggie thought it looked as though the building hadn't been completed yet: there were some scaffolds against the walls.

But it was the smells coming from the dining room that really bothered her. She was hungry, but knew enough not to ask for any food.

Finally, Manfred came and helped a "red cap" load the luggage on a cart and the two men left. When he came back, he said they had to hurry. They went down some steps and boarded a Rock Island train.

Manfred was so nervous he kept looking around until they were well clear of the yards. Baby John was soon asleep on Hedy's lap. Maggie looked out at the buildings, the rails, the trains with names on the cars—Burlington Route, Corn Belt Route, Great Northern, Northern Pacific, Peoria Gateway, Chicago and Northwestern, Chicago Milwaukee St. Paul and Pacific or sometimes just Milwaukee Road, Minneapolis St. Paul Sault Ste. Marie or just Soo Line—and dreamed of going with them, even though most of them were box cars.

Baby John woke up at Des Moines because they had to change trains, but he fell asleep again almost as soon as they got into the waiting room. Maggie was tired, but she kept her eyes on the station as they walked on the platform: it was two stories of brown brick with a large semi-circular roof on one end which people could walk under and not get rained or snowed on. She liked the sign on the wall that read "ROCK ISLAND." The waiting room wasn't nearly as big as the one in St. Paul. Just before she fell asleep, she told herself that someday she'd find that island on a map.

She woke up halfway to Omaha and didn't even remember getting on the train. At the Union Station Hedy went to call her sister, Manfred collected all the baggage, and Maggie was told to watch Baby John. She amused herself by checking the three large synchronized clocks to see if they were always on the same minute. They were.

Uncle Jerry was not happy when he pulled up to the platform and got out to help load the Voglers' possessions. Even Manfred's dismal attempt at a "thank you" didn't make him any happier.

Maggie was happy: she was with Linda Kaye again and they'd be in the same classroom. Linda Kaye had a new brother, so over the weekend Maggie and Linda Kaye spent much of their time taking care of Baby John and Jerry, Jr., pretending they were mothers of the boys.

The girls shared Linda Kaye's bed, just like in the old days, and Sunday night Linda Kaye told Maggie all about her school, her classmates, and the teacher. She made them all sound so nice Maggie couldn't wait for morning. Most of the day went well, but the end wasn't so good for Maggie because when the last bell sounded and all the students stood beside their desks before being dismissed, Maggie started saying the "Hail Mary" and the other kids laughed. Even Linda Kaye.

Hedy had to register Maggie. As part of the registration, the principal needed to know what schools Maggie had attended so she could get her records. Hedy only told her about the school in Great Falls; Manfred had warned her not to say anything about St. Matthew's or about St. Paul, for that matter.

It didn't make any difference: by the time the records arrived from Great Falls, the Voglers were in South Dakota, the result of a fist fight between Uncle Jerry and Manfred, broken up only after each wife grabbed hold of her man. The girls had been sent to their room, but they heard words such as "bootleggers," "gambling," and one bellow from Uncle Jerry about Manfred being the only Kraut stupid enough to cross both "Big Ed" Morgan and "Kid Cann" and think he could get away with it.

The next day Linda Kaye and Maggie cried when they said goodbye. Linda Kaye went to school; Maggie climbed into Uncle Jerry's car, and he drove the Voglers to the Union Station. He never said a word the entire trip, not even to Hedy. Maggie was miserable.

Manfred was stifling the anger that had been boiling up because he had to rely on his in-law's for enough money to get railroad tickets, food, and rent for a week. Hedy and Maggie recognized the danger and stayed quiet.

The train trip was a slow one. Gone were the days of riding well-kept passenger coaches. They moved in fits and starts on the locals and mixed trains of the Chicago & Northwestern in coaches that had seen better days; some of them much better days.

Manfred wanted a spot far away from the Twin Cities, a town where he could live distant from anyone who might recognize him, a place on the edge of civilization. The perfect answer was Aberdeen, South Dakota.

Manfred always wanted to rent houses, but in Aberdeen the family had to stay in a boarding house on the north side, while he got a job cooking at Northern State Teachers' College, which he saw as the worst job he'd ever had. It wasn't just that the students complained about everything he and the other cooks made; the meat, flour, canned goods, and even any fresh vegetables and fruits they had to work with were always low quality. Manfred knew that even the best chef at Delmonico's in New York City couldn't have made anything really tasty out of those raw ingredients. Delmonico's was a dream of his; he knew he'd never have enough money to own such a fabulous restaurant, but he'd been dreaming of owning a small eating establishment someday; one where he'd fill out the menu, do the cooking, and hire and fire the help.

Hedy registered Maggie in the fourth grade, but without mentioning either school in St. Paul or Omaha. When the principal concluded that Maggie had not been to school for at least two months, she had to take tests to see where she should be placed. She did well enough to stay in fourth grade, although her arithmetic was not strong.

Looking out the window of their small boarding house apartment, Maggie saw nothing but flat land and a few trees extending to the north even beyond her eyesight. Could it be possible the land was flat all the way to the North Pole?

Maggie liked variety: she liked the busy movement of people in Omaha, despite the stockyard smells that sometimes clung like a giant barnyard over the city; the state capitol in Lincoln with its columns and a large dome with a smaller dome on top of it; the trees that seemed to shelter Chaska; the railroad noises and bright lights of Great Falls; the grand view she had from her street in St. Paul of the Mississippi River below the bluffs and across the river the great dome of the Cathedral. Aberdeen seemed so blah.

When her class was given library time, Maggie found a book, *The Wizard of Oz*. When the teacher told her that Mr. Baum, the author, had lived in Aberdeen for awhile, she checked it out.

In the book the little girl named Dorothy lived on the prairie of Kansas, which the author described as gray: the soil; the grass; the house; Aunt Em's eyes, cheeks, and lips; even Uncle Henry. About the only thing that wasn't gray was the little black dog Toto.

Maggie was living on the prairie, too, although in a town, not on a farm. But she could see the countryside and it wasn't gray. Spring showed off in green and brown and there were blue skies and white clouds. She couldn't remember what it was like around Topeka, but she was certain it wasn't gray.

Other than her disagreement over the color of the prairie, Maggie enjoyed the book, even though she felt scared for Dorothy when the cyclone picked her up inside the house and took her to the land of the Munchkins, which was very colorful.

Maggie liked the drawings of Dorothy, Toto, the Munchkins, the Good Witch (she'd never heard of one being good before), and the Scarecrow. She hoped that Dorothy would get back home like she wanted and resisted the temptation to turn to the back of the book to find out if she did or not, and she wished Dorothy would get to keep the silver shoes that had belonged to the wicked Witch of the East because Maggie knew she would never have another chance to get such a fine pair of shoes. But most of all she was glad that Dorothy had found a friend, even though the Scarecrow wasn't a real human.

She didn't have time to finish the book or think much about the geography and color of prairie life, the little Munchkins, or the friendship of Dorothy and the Scarecrow, however, because Manfred was on the move again. She had just finished the chapter about the Scarecrow when the family and their valuables were loaded into the vehicle of a bachelor, another cook at the college, and headed north to Kingston, North Dakota. The driver insisted it would be a nice outing for him on a wonderful spring day; he didn't mention all the bootleg booze Manfred had treated him to.

Manfred got a job as a second cook and baker at the Royal Arms Hotel. And stayed off the booze. For a month. Then his resistance crumbled. When he came to, he was lying in the gutter outside a blind pig.

Everyone else had gone home, but someone had put a lot of newspapers over him, maybe as a blanket.

As he rolled over, his eye caught an ad. There was a restaurant for lease in the small town of Menninger. It was difficult to read with just one eye, but the other one seemed swollen as if someone had hit him there. He couldn't remember.

A Northern Pacific branch line ran from Kingston through Menninger, and a few days later Manfred was on it. He met the owner of the building, looked it over, and signed a lease. He also rented a house a block away. Two days later the Voglers were residents of Menninger.

Maggie had just about finished the fourth grade in the Kingston Elementary School and was even passing, mostly with B's and C's, but with an A in Geography.

Maggie spent the final two weeks of fourth grade in Menninger and then the school term was over. She had to walk five blocks to Guilford Street and what was called the Park School, but no one knew why. Children who lived west of the NP line went to grades 1-8 there and then transferred to the main school up on Villard. In addition to the classrooms, the building had apartments for the single lady teachers; the janitor lived in the basement.

The Voglers lived in a one-and-a-half story white frame house at the corner of Dunnell and Dakota. Dakota was nicely graveled, and Dunnell had a nice gravel overlay east of Dakota, but on the west side where it ran in front of their house, Dunnell was not much more than a dirt track. Theirs was the only home on the south half of the block.

Up the Dakota Street hill stood the Oleson House, a large hotel which was not as glamorous as it had been. Manfred's restaurant, Fred's Chop House, was next door.

Manfred wanted to provide better quality food than the burgers and hot beef sandwiches that the other restaurants on Villard and over on St. Paul featured, but it put him in direct competition with the dining rooms at the Oleson and at the Menninger Arms a block north on Lamborn. The man from whom he leased the building stopped in one day and tried to reason with him, that Menninger was just a small town with small town appetites, and he would be better off selling burgers, beans, fried chicken, mashed potatoes, and home-made pie rather than the more expensive steaks and chops he had on the menu. But Manfred knew what he wanted and continued to cook his way.

During the first few weeks of business, it appeared his gamble might pay off. Many residents of Menninger and the surrounding area stopped in and went away favorably impressed. Manfred was elated. However, workingmen, families with small children, and retired people couldn't afford to eat at the Chop House very often and business tailed off. Manfred needed consolation: he found it in a bottle. Or rather many bottles.

His drinking began to affect his cooking and even less business was the result, which led to more drinking. Even the birth of a daughter that summer didn't stop Manfred's descent into the insatiable craving for blind pig alcohol. In the past when Manfred drank, he was unpleasant and mean, but as an alcoholic, he was uncaring and cruel. Maggie soon found that out.

July in central North Dakota is usually hot and dry, but that July a freak rainstorm kicked up from the southwest and didn't stop for twenty-four hours. When Maggie went out after breakfast the next day, she was thrilled to see so much water south of Dunnell.

There was a marsh halfway between Dunnell and the Great Northern depot even further to the south. Most of the time it was a shallow, reed-choked, watery afterthought, but the storm caused it to run full with Dakota Street acting as a dam.

Maggie had been warned she was not allowed to go near the railroad. Sometimes during the day she'd watch the passenger trains as they stopped at the station and the switch engines taking care of freight cars. At night she could hear the trains, and several times she woke up and looked out the window in her attic-like bedroom and saw the glow of the fireboxes under the locomotives, the headlights, and even some lights in the passenger car windows. She told herself that someday she'd be on a train to a faraway place where M.F. could never find her. Then she would send for her mother and Johnny and her new sister Alys and they would be a family.

To the west of her house where Dunnell ended and Walcott Street went north at a right angle, there had been a wooden bridge so the railroad men who lived on the west side had easier access to the depot and yards. It had handrails, and Maggie had held onto them when she played on the bridge, but never dared cross it because then she'd be on railroad property and M.F. would thrash her.

That morning the bridge had washed away from its two approaches and ended up grounded just in front of Maggie's house. M.F. was already at the Chop House; her mother was busy with Alys; and Johnny, always a slow eater, was still at the table, so Maggie walked down to the bridge. It looked like it would make a fine raft. She went to the shed that came with the house and found a long 2x2. She stepped onto the bridge and used the 2x2 as a pole to push away from the shore. The "raft" rode low, so she threw her shoes and stockings onto the bank and polled away on an adventure.

She went to Dakota Street and then poled back to the west as far as she could go. The morning was warming and perspiration came easily. Finally, the water shallowed and the reeds thickened, so she had to turn back. Sometimes a car would go by on Villard and honk; Maggie would wave an answer.

When she got back home, Johnny was making mud pies near a puddle. He saw her and ran to the water. When she pulled in, he said, "Me, too," and indicated the raft. Maggie got off and helped him wash his hands in the marsh water; then they went into the house.

Maggie was thirsty and drank some water. Her mother had finished nursing Alys and was resting. Maggie said that she and Johnny would be playing outside. Without looking up, her mother told her that would be all right, but not too far away.

On her way out, Maggie took a day-old roll from the restaurant and ate it as she and Johnny went to the raft. After he took off his shoes and socks and got aboard, Maggie worried he might slip off, so she went to the shed and came back with a length of twine. She tied him to a handrail and poled off. She tested the motion. The raft was long enough and wide enough that there was no danger of capsizing, so she got braver and off they went to the west.

Maggie would point out things to Johnny: the approaches where the bridge had been; the black water tower for the steam locomotives off to the south; a hump of mud, twigs, and reeds that some animal had made for a home, but most of it was beneath the flood water; some birds' nests hidden among the reeds; and above it all the warning cries of the red-winged blackbirds. Some of them came close to the raft and Johnny was scared, but Maggie said they weren't going to peck him; they were scared, too.

On the way back the children saw a brown furry animal swimming out of the reeds into the clear channel. Its smooth ratty tail followed like a dark snake. Johnny started to cry, but Maggie said, "Aww, that's just a darn old mush rat; he won't hurt yuh." The animal disappeared beneath the surface and Johnny smiled up at Maggie. She was so smart.

It took a long time, but finally Maggie had the raft at Dakota Street. The town drunk, Hiram, and his black lab, Jack Johnson, were walking on the sidewalk.

"Hey, yuh, Maggie; takin' yur little brother on a trip, I see."

"Yeah, but it's time to go home. We were way out west."

As she poled away from the street, Jack Johnson jumped into the water, swam to the raft, and tried to climb aboard. He couldn't, so he swam around the raft and started back to Hiram, who was doubled over with laughter and slapping his thigh at JJ's antics. Both Maggie and Johnny patted JJ as his black head slipped past.

Manfred's morning had been a bad one. He'd gotten a bottle of booze the night before from Tillie Mortensen, a notorious blind pig, and had been nipping on it. It wasn't even noon, and he had to call in his assistant cook so he could go home and rest for awhile.

As he was walking down Dakota, chewing a cigar, he met Hiram and his black dog.

"Mornin', Mr. Vogler. That's quite a pair of youngin's yuh have. I hope they don't get wet."

Manfred didn't say a word: he had no idea what Hiram was talking about. Then as he came around the corner of his house, he saw the raft and that the son who would replace his brother was in danger of drowning.

He reached the bank just as Maggie was untying Johnny. She was proud of the way she had protected Johnny while on the adventure.

Manfred threw Johnny into the crook of his arm and grabbed Maggie's wrist so tightly she started to cry. He rushed the children into the house and began yelling at Hedy for not watching them closely enough. Alys began to cry; Johnny joined in.

Manfred pulled off his belt and started to beat Maggie, the leather hissing through the air. Once again, no supper. Her mother put salve on her savaged bottom.

Maggie had been getting spankings a couple times a week since Manfred's business started to decline: her room was a mess; she wasn't helping her mother enough; she spilled her milk at the table; she tore her dress; she even got spanked once for staring out the window during supper instead of eating.

A week after the beating Manfred came up with an idea after he tried to get easier terms on the restaurant lease from the building owner without success. If he brought the owner home to a meal, the man would see his little children and relent.

On Friday he left the Chop House early and prepared an expensive meal with ingredients his family never enjoyed. Maggie smelled the food cooking and could hardly wait to taste it.

The man was supposed to show up at six o'clock. At 5:45 Manfred pulled Maggie aside and had her sit on the davenport. He stared down at her. "Margarete, an important man vill be at supper. You vill be at der table with good manners. He hass a very…a large…odt nose. Do not notice it. Do not ask about it. You must do vhat I say. Iss that understood?"

"Yes."

"Yes, what?"

"Yes, sir."

"Remember to say that to him at supper, but only if he talks to you."

When the man came in, Manfred took his hat and then introduced him to Hedy and the children. Then Hedy led Johnny away; they would eat in a little room upstairs and Hedy would nurse Alys. Maggie was nervous.

The food was delicious. Maggie had heard M.F. was a good cook, and now it was confirmed, but there was not total enjoyment for her: she knew she shouldn't stare at the visitor's nose, but found that she couldn't help it.

A few years before, a horse had kicked the man square in the face. He was unconscious for two days, but then recovered. All except his nose. It lay over on the side of his face like a large piece of purple-veined sausage. Maggie had never seen anything like it. At first, she kept her head down and ate, but then the man asked what grade she would be in, and after she answered, her father told her to look at the man when he was speaking to her.

After that she was lost. Even though she was only peeking at the nose occasionally, she caught M.F.'s eye enough times to know that he was furious. At the end of the evening and cigars, the man still turned Manfred's request down. When the man left, Manfred knew it was Maggie's fault for staring.

He went to the bathroom and got his razor strop. On one end there was a hard leather handle; on the other there was a metal ring. Maggie had never been stropped before, so she didn't know what M.F. was doing as he approached her. He grabbed and pushed her face onto the davenport. She knew what was coming then and prepared her count. Sometimes he whacked her bottom three or four times; the most he'd ever done was twelve after the raft incident. No matter the number, counting the blows helped her endure and not cry out.

Suddenly he pulled up her dress and ripped off her underwear. Before she could react to this new thing, he had formed a fist around the leather handle and began flailing his daughter.

"Du kleine Schlampe! You little bitch! You've ruined me! Schlampe!"

Maggie had no chance to count; the combination of the pain and the fact she couldn't breathe made her pass out.

The beating might have continued until Maggie was dead, but suddenly Hedy was there and threw her body across that of her daughter. The strop struck her in the back and the pain forced a shriek from her mouth.

The red veil lifted from Manfred's eyes. His sobbing wife, his little girl's blood; he threw the red-stained strop on the floor and ran out into the night.

Hedy had been raised in a strict German family where "Der vater ist der chef." In English that meant "The father is the boss," but that does not really convey the power those words placed in the father's hands. Not the authority of the old Roman fathers who had the power of life and death over their sons and daughters, but mighty close.

When Hedy had heard Manfred's thunderous voice, she raced for the stairs. Halfway down she saw that he was killing Maggie; blood was flying everywhere: the davenport, the floor, Maggie's dress. Manfred's hand looked just like it did when he was killing and butchering pigs.

When she was certain that Maggie was breathing, she got two blankets from the chest and put one under and one over her frail body. Then she called the Oleson House, where Doc Blanchard lived. He wasn't the best doctor in town, but he was the closest. Her next call was to the chief of police.

The Voglers had no car, no Victrola, no stereopticon, no radio, not even a washing machine or vacuum cleaner, but they did have a telephone. And that probably saved Maggie's life.

Doc hustled in with his black bag and went right to work. Maggie was torn and ripped from her thighs to the small of her back. She came to when Doc was applying some dressings; tears rolled down her cheeks, but she didn't utter a sound.

When the chief of police showed up, he took a brief look at Maggie, heard Hedy say that Manfred had done it, told her something, and headed back uptown.

The chief sat in his office in the city hall on Lamborn. He was pretty certain Manfred was in a blind pig, but it wouldn't look right for the police chief to go into an illegal establishment and arrest a patron without shutting the whole place down, so he told Officer Hagen to locate Hiram. When Hiram came in, he sent him after Manfred.

Hiram checked the blind pigs on St. Paul and then moved west of the tracks, where he found Manfred at Tillie's, loaded and legless. He reported to the chief, who sent Officer Hagen over to Tillie's. Hagen had two men carry Manfred the half block to the city hall, where he was placed under arrest and jailed. He slept the night away.

The next morning the chief drove him down Dakota. Manfred thanked him, but didn't know what to say when they came to the front door where three suitcases full of Manfred's things were sitting. The chief explained that Manfred was leaving town, and if he returned, he'd be up on serious charges that would lead to prison. He loaded the suitcases in the car and ordered Manfred to follow. Hedy never appeared.

The chief drove to the depot and made certain Manfred bought a ticket. He said he'd check after the passenger train had pulled out and Manfred had better be on it. When he went to the station later on, Manfred was gone.

Doc Blanchard showed Hedy how to change the dressings and keep the wounds clean. Maggie slowly made a recovery, with only slight scarring where the metal had bitten the deepest. She missed a circus and a carnival, but there wouldn't have been money for tickets anyway, and she did get to look out her window as the circus wagons were unloaded from their flat cars on the spur line by the depot and move up the Dakota Street hill, pulled by the elephants.

First came the band wagon, blaring out brassy music, then the wild animals in their cages—lions, tigers, leopards, baboons, monkeys, a large brown bear, a sign reading "Hippopotamus," but it was in a tank of water and she couldn't see it; Maggie tried to remember the countries where such beasts lived. The Big Top canvas and its poles. Camels and horses ridden by "Arabs" and beautifully costumed girls. A man on stilts, with long pants covering the wood and dressed like Uncle Sam. A couple dozen clowns and other circus performers. When the last of them passed out of view, Maggie felt like she had actually been at a circus.

Faced with no income, Hedy took over the Chop House, changing the name to Hedy's Haven and cooking all the small-town fare Manfred had refused to serve. Slowly her customer base increased, partly because she was a good cook and partly because the people of Menninger knew what a rotten husband she had.

The fifth grade was the best one yet for Maggie, completely healed by the time school rolled around. Her teacher was Miss Abigail Fenton, a first-year teacher from Minot. She had both the fifth and the sixth graders in one room, and she had that new-teacher determination that she could make a difference in the lives of her students and, in turn, they would make a difference in the world. It was only later that the patina of disappointments would glaze her hope-filled outlook and turn it into the cynicism of so many older educators.

Miss Fenton encouraged all her students, but especially the ones that were damaged physically or emotionally: the slow boy nicknamed Antsy from across the river; Esther, the little girl that had to wear a brace on her right leg; Barry, the overweight boy with the speech impediment and so far behind in academic skills; and Maggie, whose father was such a monster.

Every student made some progress that year, not because they liked learning (it was hard), but because they liked Miss Fenton and didn't want to disappoint her.

Maggie loved Miss Fenton and prayed for her every night, especially since her mother was taking the family to the white wooden German Lutheran Church three blocks up Dunnell now that Manfred was gone. Miss Fenton encouraged all her students to develop their skills and abilities. She saw how much Maggie liked geography and literature, especially since her reading was rapidly improving, and she was quick to introduce Maggie to books she might be interested in.

At Christmas time Maggie brought Miss Fenton two sweet rolls her mother had baked; Miss Fenton had a little present for each student: the boys all got six fish hooks; Maggie and the girls each received a small handkerchief.

That was the Christmas Maggie learned she was poor. It was something that had never occurred to her. Of course, the daughters in the better-off families kept their friendships among themselves, but there weren't that many rich families west of the tracks, so Maggie wasn't jealous. While Maggie's dresses and shoes weren't the best and often were second-hand, they were clean and not any worse than those worn by her friends Aggie and Hilda and freckle-faced Tillie, and Maggie never thought of her friends as poor.

A couple days into Christmas vacation, the house was alive with the smell of baked goods—all kinds of Christmas cookies, sweet rolls, butter horns, a couple cakes, and a big pan of fudge. Hedy wrapped some of the cookies, sweet rolls, a piece of cake, and some fudge in waxed paper and placed it in a box with a cover.

"Maggie, I want you to take this to Mrs. Landsteiner. Be sure to button your coat all the way; it's chilly."

"Yes, Mama."

Mrs. Landsteiner was an old widow lady that lived in a little house three blocks away on Stimson. She was German-Bohemian so Mama could talk with her, but it was hard for Maggie to figure out what she was saying because her accented English was not too good. Sometimes when Maggie walked down to Tillie's house on Park Avenue near the river, she would see Mrs. Landsteiner in her garden. She would poke her cane into the soil so it would stand by itself, then she'd bend over and hoe a little ways, then stab her cane in again and move on. In her kerchief and long dress, she reminded Maggie of the three peasant women in the picture "The Gleaners" on the wall of Miss Fenton's room. They were bent over, picking up left-over wheat in a harvested field. Maggie felt sorry for them.

When Maggie was ready, Mama said, "Just put it on her steps and leave. Don't knock. Understand, mein schatz?"

"Yes, Mama, but why not knock?"

"It's a sort of Christmas present we are giving. Mrs. Landsteiner does not have much money, so we help her a little to have a happy Christmas. Understand?"

"Yes, Mama."

When Maggie opened the door, she almost knocked an old lady down. She had just left a box on the steps and was straightening up. Maggie saw it was Mrs. Landsteiner. Maggie blushed, she was so embarrassed; Mrs. Landsteiner was embarrassed, too. She exclaimed, "Donnerwetter!" and hobbled off the steps.

Maggie waited until she had gone around the corner of the house, then she brought the box to Mama. Mama took out a fruitcake called Stollen, a German gingerbread called Lebkuchen, and several kinds of German Christmas cookies—Spekulatius, Vanillekipferi, butter cookies, and hazelnut macaroons.

Mama started to laugh; it was good to see her laugh.

"Why are you laughing, Mama?"

"It seems we have a Christmas present of our own, meine kleine maus."

She laughed even harder when Maggie told her what Mrs. Landsteiner had said. When Maggie asked what it meant, Mama said, "Thunderstorm," and laughed even more.

That afternoon Maggie was still wondering what was so funny when she put her box on Mrs. Landsteiner's steps and ran away.

During the school year Hedy would take Johnny and Alys to the restaurant and keep them there, usually in a small room off the kitchen area. When school let out, they were Maggie's responsibility, although Hedy would walk down the hill to nurse Alys several times a day. Maggie didn't mind; she loved her brother and sister.

Hedy had a fence put up, so Johnny didn't have to be in the house all the time. She also made sure that Maggie had some time to be with her friends. They'd play hide-and-seek, anti-i-over, or kick the can if it was dark enough. Tillie (her name was Mathilda which she didn't like, and she didn't even mind if the kids teased her about being Tillie Mortensen's long-lost daughter) had been eight years old when she fell out of the hay loft door in a barn where she and her brothers were playing and suffered a compound fracture of her left leg. Although the doctor did the best he could, the leg never was right, and she couldn't walk or run as fast as the other kids. Still she was Maggie's friend: she was funny, never said hurtful things, and never complained about her leg.

On Tillie's birthday she treated her friends to a movie at the Blackstone. It was *Nice People*, a comedy starring Wallace Reid and Bebe Daniels, and it was Maggie's first movie. She left the theater with a crush on handsome Wallace Reid. It was several months before her mother told her that Wallace Reid had died. Hedy didn't tell Maggie it was from drug addiction.

The summer went swiftly and then it was sixth grade and Miss Fenton.

Two weeks into school, Hedy received a letter which would wreck Maggie's new-found idyllic life.

It was from Manfred. He had taken the pledge and no longer drank. He had found religion and Christ was his savior. He had a good-paying job as second cook and baker at the Powers Hotel at Broadway and 4th in Fargo. He loved Hedy and his children very much, was sorry for all his past sinful acts, and wanted them to join him so they could be a family again.

A cashier's check was enclosed for travel expenses.

Hedy was certain she saw tear stains on the paper.

After much agonizing Hedy decided to go to Fargo. Maybe a tiny piece of her still loved the man he used to be. Maybe she felt her children needed a father (he did say he had reformed). Maybe her new-found Christian belief in forgiveness motivated her. Maybe it was all of those things or maybe none of them.

When she told Maggie they were moving to Fargo, Maggie's heart formed a hole that all the love Hedy had for her couldn't fill it.

On her last day in the Park School, Maggie said goodbye to her friends in the hallway amidst a sudden rush of tears.

The three had drawn a picture for Maggie. Each girl drew and colored herself, and they all filled in the dresses in their favorite colors. Then all three helped to draw Maggie and they colored her dress yellow.

Across the top they printed "We love you." Across the bottom was "WE'LL MISS YOU MAGGIE" with her name squished together because they had run out of room.

Seeing the picture with Aggie in blue, Hilda in purple, and Tillie in green made Maggie cry even harder. Under each figure was a name, but if anyone knew the girls, it was easy to pick out who was who without the names, even though the Tillie figure didn't have a bent left leg.

Tears were coming down the cheeks of all the girl-figures; they looked like blue scars on the paper faces.

After the miserable group of little girls broke apart and the others walked slowly down the stairway, Maggie ran to the lavatory to wash her face and went back in to tell Miss Fenton goodbye. She handed Miss

Fenton the library book she'd been reading, and Miss Fenton laughed as she looked at it. "Where did you find this, Maggie?"

"It was in the back of the geography section; someone must have shoved it back there. I found it."

"Well, you're such a good finder, I think you should keep it. It's over forty years old and outdated, so I don't think the school will miss it…and when you come back, you can turn the book in then. All right?"

Maggie wasn't sure about taking something that didn't belong to her, but if Miss Fenton said it was all right, it must be all right. She nodded. Miss Fenton then handed her a small package and said. "This will remind you of the good times here at Park School. You can open it at home." There was a hug, some tears, and Maggie headed out the door.

In her room at home, she opened the package and saw a thin bracelet. She knew it wasn't silver, but she pretended that it was. It was the first jewelry Maggie ever owned.

When she showed her mother, Hedy commented on how nice it looked on her and about how nice Miss Fenton was.

It wasn't until the train had started that Hedy told her that the family would be together; they'd be living with Papa again. If Maggie could have jumped off the train, she would have. Instead, she buried her face in the cushion which absorbed her tears. Even the bracelet didn't help. She didn't feel close to her mother again for a long time.

At first, everything went well. Manfred was sober, sorry, and solicitous. They had a house that bordered downtown Fargo; her school—she wasn't certain of the name, either Longfellow or Douglas Terrace, she'd heard both—was only ten blocks away; and she had a new friend.

Maggie soon discovered that there was a tiny building on the alley behind their house; it probably started out as a stable. When she went exploring, she was surprised to see a little woman come out of the boxy house. Maggie had been growing and all her walking helped build her muscles, so even though she was only eleven she was a foot taller and much larger than the woman.

They stared at each other, then the woman spoke. "Hi, my name is Dorothea, but don't call me that because people say 'Dorothea the Dwarf,' and I don't like that."

"What should I call you then?"

"I like 'Rosie'; it was my mother's name."

"Rosie, then; I'm Maggie. We just moved in."

"I know; I saw you."

"Well, I'm glad to know you, Rosie, but I'm exploring my new neighborhood. Goodbye."

"Bye. Be careful; there are some mean boys around. Stop over some time."

Maggie didn't run into any mean boys; the ones at her school were all right, but didn't have much to do with girls, except the eighth grade ones. There were lots of girls, but Maggie was shy about meeting them. Her new teacher, Miss Gregg, was all right, but she was no Miss Fenton.

Maggie began to withdraw from her classmates and even her family. She hated being around M.F., so she spent as much time as possible in her room.

After a particularly lonely day, she decided to go see Rosie. After Rosie got over her surprise, she invited Maggie into a house unlike any she'd ever been in. Rosie's house had chairs, table, bed, heating stove in the middle of the room, cooking stove, sink, step-stool, the smallest ice box imaginable, a beat-up chifforobe, and a screen which hid the bathroom facilities, all crammed into one big room. (All the houses in Fargo had water and sewer, unlike some of those in Menninger.) But the really strange thing was that the walls were hidden by stacks of newspapers.

As they talked at the table, with the sunlight drifting through a cloudy window, Maggie realized she was making a new friend. And that she would like to come again.

Over the next few weeks Maggie told Rosie about herself and Rosie returned the compliment. Her parents had been regular-size people, but they were dead. She had graduated eighth grade, but didn't like the way the school kids teased her, calling her a midget, a dwarf, short cake, small stuff, some things she wouldn't repeat, and were always rubbing her head for "luck," so she got a job on probation helping to clean a big hotel in Fargo.

She first talked with Edward Cole, who owned the first-class Metropole Hotel on NP Avenue. When she asked for a job as housekeeper, he laughed, and that didn't make her feel very good. But she had heard that Cole was a big Democrat, so she told him she liked William Jennings Bryan, then he stopped laughing and gave her a trial job at a second-class hotel he also owned, the Cole, a block down NP from the Metropole.

Cole was so pleased with her efficiency and thoroughness, he moved her over to the Metropole and recommended her to his hotel-owner friends. So she had worked at the Waldorf at Front and 7th, the Continental on Broadway and 2nd, the Fargo House on Front, and the Gardner at Roberts and 1st. Sometimes two at a time. She was very choosy and wouldn't work at the Dixon, the Hotel Annex, or the Hotel Donaldson because the railroad men and the laborers who frequented them were so mean to her. Maggie didn't know Fargo very well, so the street names didn't mean much to her, but she liked the fact that Rosie was somewhat geographically minded.

Rosie was proud of the fact she had never missed a day of work, even climbing over snow drifts taller than she was to make sure that rooms were cleaned. She treasured the bonuses her bosses gave her at Christmas time, including a little Christmas tree from Mr. Cole.

One Saturday, Rosie got a mischievous twinkle in her eye, and said, "Maggie, I want to show you my hobby." She popped off her chair and signaled Maggie to follow her to several stacks of newspapers. Rosie had newspapers stacked against her walls under the sink and on a shelf over it, up to the bottom of her two windows and on shelves above them, everywhere except behind the cook stove. "The papers help keep my house warm. My first few winters here were so cold." She hugged herself and shivered. "When I find a newspaper someone threw out in a hotel, I take it home and use it in my stacks. I have so many newspapers now I am throwing away some of my early ones…except for these." She went behind the screen and emerged, lugging a step ladder. She angled out the legs and climbed to the top of a stack made up of folded single sheets.

On the floor again, she said, "Look." Maggie saw a single page of newspaper.

Maggie wasn't familiar with newspapers; M.F. didn't like them and only bought one when he was searching for a job, although in Menninger he would occasionally read the German-language newspaper out of Bismarck, *Der Staats Anzeiger*.

What Maggie saw amazed her: the page was covered with drawings of people, animals, buildings, cars, trees, the sky, and there were words above the characters' heads, so she knew what each character said, unlike the silent movie she had seen.

Rosie called them the comics; some of them were from Fargo papers and others from papers in the Twin Cities. There were even some from Chicago. She would cut off the comics page and put those in separate stacks. Rosie went up the ladder and began handing more comics down to Maggie.

Rosie spread a page on the table in front of Maggie, pointed at one of the strips and said, "This is my favorite." Maggie saw it was called *Winnie Winkle, The Breadwinner*. Rosie let her read the strip and then placed other pages on the table, so Maggie could get the gist of the story of Winnie, a young, blonde, working woman who was supporting her mother, bald-headed father, and younger brother. The strip contained gags and humorous situations.

While Maggie was reading, Rosie went to a different stack and put a Sunday comics section in front of Maggie. It was in color; Maggie could hardly believe her eyes.

Rosie didn't like the Sunday Winnie strips as much because they were mostly about Perry, the little brother, and his friends.

She also liked *Harold Teen* and *Gasoline Alley*.

"If the boys at school had been as nice as Harold, I wouldn't have quit. He's so nice to everyone, especially to his girl Lillums. Wouldn't you like to go to the Sugar Bowl and have a chocolate soda with them?"

Maggie supposed that she would.

"I didn't used to like *Gasoline Alley*, 'cause they seemed always to be tinkerin' with some automobile, but a couple years ago someone left a little baby on Walt Wallet's doorstep. He was a bachelor, but he kept the baby and named him Skeezix. Isn't that a funny name? I know Skeezix grew from a baby to a boy faster than real babies do, but now the Wallets are a family. I like that."

Maggie thought it somewhat strange that Rosie would like Walt Wallet, who had a hugely overweight body, but he was kind and friendly to folks, so Maggie could see Rosie's point of view.

Rosie also liked *Moon Mullins* and *Smitty*. Moon was a roughneck who always seemed to be getting into fights, which didn't bother Rosie that much because they weren't like real fist fights and always ended with a joke or humor of some type. Rosie's favorite character was Moon's kid brother Kayo, who always sported an oversized black derby. *Smitty* was about a freckle-faced office boy who was in short pants and wore a bow tie. Rosie liked the fact that he was small, just like she was.

There was one strip that Rosie didn't care for—*The Gumps*. After she read a few strips, neither did Maggie. The drawing wasn't very good, and Andy Gump and his Uncle Bim were drawn without chins, which made Maggie feel uneasy.

After they had spent a half hour or so looking at comic strips, Rosie went over to the chifforobe and took out a Sunday comic section from the *New York Daily News* of November 2, 1924, the only one in her collection from that paper. Rosie said, "Here's one of my favorites, but it's the only one I have so far."

The strip was called *Little Orphan Annie* and was about a red-haired orphan girl who couldn't have ice cream for dessert because she hadn't made her bed properly. The other orphans teased her about having to eat mush and milk, so she chased them out of the dining room and vowed to get the next one who teased her. When she heard someone coming in the room, she threw her bowl of mush and hit Miss Asthma, the orphanage director, right in the face. In the last panel Miss Asthma was chasing Annie around the table with a stick.

"I like Annie; she has gumption. I think she can take care of herself, don't you?"

Maggie did.

"I'd like to be able to take care of myself the way Annie does. I hope I can find more of her strips."

It was time to put away the comics, but before Maggie left, Rosie asked, "What are your hobbies, Maggie."

"I read. Someday I'll show you my book."

As Maggie walked home, she realized that compared to Rosie, she didn't have much of a hobby. She had answered on the spur of the moment, but as she thought about it, reading was her hobby, her only one. She couldn't count baking, even though her mother had shown her how to make bread, rolls, cookies, cakes, and fudge, which all tasted good. And washing clothes with a wash board and wash tub and doing such a good job her mother even said she couldn't have done any better wasn't a hobby. Nor was cleaning house; nor taking care of Johnny and Alys. No, it had to be reading.

A week or so later Maggie brought her geography book to Rosie's and they looked at it. The book was so old Rosie was afraid to turn the pages for fear they would tear, but Maggie reassured her. "It's all right; some of the pages are torn already. Miss Fenton says books are meant to be read, so if we don't turn the pages, how can we read the book?"

Rosie was a good reader, and while Maggie coached her on some of the words, such as "sphere," "polyps," "atolls," and "isthmus," they started on some of the lessons about the Earth, the hemispheres, and land forms. But what they both liked were the colored maps.

Of course, some of them were out of date: the U.S. map had North and South Dakota lumped together as Dakota Territory, and Oklahoma was called "Indian Territory." Prescott was still shown as the capital of Arizona Territory. Maggie knew that Arizona had become a state. Panama was still part of Columbia. Bolivia and Ecuador had much different boundaries. And Central Europe had changed so much since the Great War that Maggie didn't want Rosie even to look at that map. As for Africa, well…not that Maggie knew all that much about the countries there, but she knew enough to tell Rosie not to believe any of the political divisions, although the physical map with lakes, rivers, mountains, and deserts was all right.

Rosie marveled at the maps and the drawings of animals and people from all over the world. She was picking up so much knowledge from the lessons that Maggie thought she would like to become a teacher, just like Miss Fenton.

After a few more visits with Rosie and the book, she was certain of it and hoped there'd be money for college someday.

At night in addition to Miss Fenton, Maggie included Miss Anna Dickson in her prayers.

On Maggie's twelfth birthday, she brought some cake to Rosie, and they ate cake and read comics and studied geography together.

That spring was a big one for the Voglers. Manfred had been given an opportunity to become the head chef at the Powers, but he would have to prepare a banquet for the mayor and several other dignitaries before the owner, Thomas F. Powers, gave his final approval. Hedy had joined a church group and she was going to be nominated as the Recording Secretary. There would be no opposition.

The problem was that Hedy's meeting corresponded with the monthly Happy Birthday celebration at which all members with birthdays that month were honored with a little party and refreshments. The official meeting would begin at three o'clock, but with the election and the party, Hedy wouldn't be able to get home before six.

That day Manfred had to be at the Powers no later than four in order to have his staff ready and his food prepared on time.

That meant Maggie had to be in the house within fifteen minutes of school dismissal so she could watch Johnny and Alys until her mother got home.

Everything may have worked out, except that Manfred had gone back to his old crutch, liquor.

After Mr. Powers told Manfred the head chef was moving to a large hotel in Minneapolis, and that the job might be his, the pressure built up beyond his ability to withstand it. The test meal was three weeks away— three weeks!—Manfred needed something to calm his nerves. He went to a blind pig on Front Street and bought a little bravery in a bottle. He kept it hidden and only took a nip when he needed one.

The closer the deadline came, the more the need developed. Soon he had three bottles hidden away.

After Hedy left on the fateful afternoon, Manfred pulled the shades on Johnny and Alys and told them to take a nap. He went downstairs, retrieved a bottle from the wood shed, and sat in his chair to review everything he had to do to make his debut as chef a success.

Trying to keep every aspect straight was agonizing; he took a drink. What if he overdid the roast beef? He took another. What if the soup was too salty or the lettuce wilty? He took another. What if Maggie didn't get home on time? He tipped the bottle, swigged it until it was dry, and reached for a second one.

Maggie knew what she had to do. Even though she hated M.F., if he got to be head chef, he would make more money for her mother, Johnny, and Alys. She watched the clock and waited for the dismissal bell. As soon as Miss Gregg said, "You're excused," Maggie was heading out of the school and straight for home.

She moved fast and in record time was crossing the NP tracks and onto Front Street. Only three blocks to go.

Down Front Street she saw a commotion of some kind. There were a lot of kids, mostly older boys, shouting at someone backed up against an empty building, hidden in the shadow of a roll-up awning. Maggie turned to move on when she recognized the "someone" as Rosie. She ran as fast as she could to the group.

The kids were yelling bad things at Rosie, making fun of her size, and calling her names, even names that didn't make any sense to Maggie like "witch," "leprechaun," "ugly dog," and "banshee." Rosie was none of those.

Maggie forced her way through the crowd. Some of the boys were pushing Rosie back against the building any time she tried to get away. Rosie wasn't saying anything, but she was so frustrated and angry that her tears were uncontrollable.

Maggie pushed past the last of the boys and put an arm around Rosie. She held up her hand and told the boys to go away. They just hooted and jeered. Rosie clung to her. Maggie kept telling the boys to leave, but they drowned her out with their yells.

"Why d'ya protect the dwarf, girlie? What's she to you, your mother?" The crowd laughed.

Maggie faced the boy, the biggest boy in the crowd. His cap was a broken-down affair, crushed onto his head. "No. She's my friend." Again the laughs, but crueler.

Maggie decided she had to do something besides talk. She let Rosie go and pushed the large boy, who fell back against some of his friends, but did not go down. He doubled his fists and came at her. Maggie doubled her fists and stood her ground.

An unwritten law says that men do not strike women, boys do not hit girls. Looking at the determination that Maggie showed made the boy hesitate. He realized she wouldn't back down. He looked for a way out: he didn't want to hit a girl, especially one smaller than he was. Finally, he said, "Let the two old witches go. We've had our fun for today. Let's go under the bridge."

If the other kids were disappointed, they didn't show it. They yelled their agreement with the bridge idea and took off. The big boy had one last trick, however: he shot out his hand, tore off Maggie's bracelet, and went ripping down the street, his other hand keeping the cap riding on his skull. The whole gang was whooping and hollering. Maggie decided she'd have to let the bracelet go and stay with Rosie.

"Thank you ever so much, Maggie. I don't know how I would've gotten out of that mess by myself. And it was my own fault. I've seen that gang before and always stayed out of their way, but today I decided to be Little Orphan Annie. You're the real Orphan Annie."

Knowing she'd made the right choice, Maggie took her hand and the two friends walked to Rosie's house. They passed wooden false-front buildings, the three-story brick Dakota Business College, more brick buildings, a turn to the right, and a yellow brick apartment house showed up on the left, a turn south past the red brick Methodist Church, another yellow brick building, a row of two-story frame houses, the Cass County Court House, a turn down an alley, and home.

"I guess being Little Orphan Annie isn't as easy as it looks." Rosie began to laugh. When Maggie saw that she'd be all right, she joined in.

It was only after Maggie saw Rosie safely in her house that she remembered she was supposed to be home.

She slipped into the house, trying not to make a sound, but it was all for nothing because M.F. glared at her from his chair.

"I'm sorry. Rosie needed me…" she began.

"Sshhutup, sei Teufel!" He stood up and wobbled back into his chair. Maggie saw he was drunk. He pushed his way out of the chair. "C'mere, you liddle Devil!" He unbuckled his belt. Maggie screamed and ran up the stairs to her room and locked the door. There was no real place to hide, so she crawled under her bed.

There was a crunching sound and the splintered door, ripped from its hinges, thumped onto the floor. Maggie saw M.F.'s feet as he entered the room. He was puffing and each puff brought forth a curse.

That Christmas Maggie had received the first doll she'd ever had. It was a Raggedy Ann doll with red yarn hair, a painted-on face, a blue dress, and a white apron. She had been planning to show it to Rosie, but hadn't gotten around to it.

When Maggie wasn't playing with the doll, she put her in a wooden apple crate with a scrap of cloth for a blanket. She could see the end of the crate; it had an anchor on the label which read "Anchor Brand Washington State Apples." She also saw M.F. trip over the crate and sprawl on the floor.

As he swore and turned his head, he saw Maggie under the bed and against the far wall. He moved himself slowly under the bed until he could grab her ankle, then he began pulling. Maggie screamed.

When she was completely out, he slapped her across the face so hard that she fell on the floor. She rolled onto her stomach and tried to stand. Manfred picked up the apple crate, shook out the doll and cloth, and smashed it down on the back of his daughter's head. The wood was the thickest on the ends of the crate and when the end hit Maggie, it gashed her to the bone. Unconsciousness was a relief. Manfred then pounded the crate into her shoulders and back until it had splintered into kindling. The red veil lifted.

When Manfred turned, he saw Johnny in the doorway, tears rolling down his cheeks, but there was no sound.

Manfred knew he had to get to work; he was going to be head chef. "Take…take care of your…ssisster." Then he left.

When Hedy walked in the front door, she was bubbling over with good news: Maggie would be so proud of her when she told about all the nice things the ladies had said about her during the nomination process.

Why were there no lights on? She got a burning pain in her stomach. She called out and thought she heard a little voice upstairs. Alys was crying in her crib; Hedy hurried to pick her up.

When she got to Maggie's room, she saw her son and daughter in a pool of red. Johnny was dabbing at his sister's head with the cloth she used for her doll blanket. There was so much to do, Hedy didn't know where to begin.

She put Alys on the bed and shooed Johnny downstairs. After checking to see that Maggie was still breathing, she put her on the bed, picked up Alys, and went downstairs to the phone. First, she asked the Central operator to put her through to the doctor that had seen Johnny when he had the croup and then to the police.

Just as she put the "candlestick" phone down, she heard a knock at the door. When she opened it, there stood the little woman who lived on the alley. Maggie had said she liked her. "May I see Maggie?"

After explaining the situation, Hedy waited for the little woman to leave, but she insisted she could help, so Hedy had her stay with Alys and Johnny while she went to her daughter's bedside and waited.

When the doctor arrived, he thought Hedy had been hurt also because there was a cross in blood on her forehead. It wasn't a cut: Hedy had dipped her finger in Maggie's blood and made the cross with it, vowing that Manfred would never touch Maggie again.

Maggie's skull was not fractured, but she would have to remain in bed for awhile; the doctor would check on her every day. After dressings and bandages, he hurried out.

By the time the police arrived and checked out the scene, Manfred was already under arrest—drunk and disorderly.

On his way out the door, he'd grabbed his last bottle of hooch and by the time he'd hit Front Street, it was gone. He wobbled down to Broadway and Front, felt an urge, and threw up in the doorway of an empty building. Feeling better, he turned north; he still had time. He could be a chef.

He staggered across the NP tracks. He had to rest; he lay down in a deserted doorway and slept.

His sleep didn't last long. When he opened his eyes, he saw an Indian with a bow in his hand and three feathers sticking up from his head, standing on a pedestal. It took him awhile to figure out it was the statue just south of the tracks and wasn't dangerous. Then he remembered he had something to do. What was it? Oh, yes, become a chef. He started up Broadway again, past NP Avenue, wobbling from side-to-side.

It was one thing for the residents of Fargo to put up with derelicts, stumblebums, dehorn drinkers, and alkies on Front Street, the east end of NP near the river, or 2nd Street, but when one of them invaded the temple of merchandising progress by daring to stumble up Broadway, that was too much. Two different couples shied away from Manfred and his babbling about cooking roast beef and both called the police.

Fargo's finest found him passed out in another doorway two blocks from the Powers. After the report on Maggie came in, the D&D became assault and battery and the ensuing bail was so high Manfred could not raise it, especially since Hedy would have nothing to do with him.

When Rosie wasn't working, she spent her time by Maggie's bed. That gave Hedy time to make certain arrangements. She sent letters to her former landlord about the house in Menninger and to the owner of the restaurant building there. When she received their answers, she made ready to move back.

Maggie missed two weeks of school, but she got to read many of Rosie's comic strips, and the two of them studied the geography book. Rosie liked to put her finger on a city and trace a route to another faraway place, even though no roads were indicated.

One day Rosie came in with something wrapped in butcher paper with a battered ribbon on it. "Here. I brought you a present."

When Maggie took off the paper there was Orphan Annie. Maggie didn't know what to say; the two hugged. Then they read the comic strip together.

On the day the family was to leave for Menninger, Maggie went to say goodbye. It was a sad one, but the tears stayed away because both of them knew leaving was for the best. As Maggie turned to leave, she handed a flat box to Rosie. "Don't open this until I've gone, O.K.?"

"All right, but I don't have anything to give you."

"You already have."

"What?"

"You're my friend."

It was only a few blocks to the NP depot, and the family got to ride in the Buick that belonged to a couple from the church. The husband loaded and unloaded the luggage. Goodbyes were said, the train was boarded, and Maggie sat by a window.

That time she looked out to see what the geography was like, even though it all seemed pretty flat.

She was looking forward to her old house, the marsh, her three friends. She hoped they remembered her and were still her friends.

The rhythm of the train made her feel sleepy. She could hardly wait to see Miss Fenton, even though she would have her only a few weeks. She hoped Miss Fenton wouldn't be too angry about losing her bracelet and not returning the geography book....

LIFE ON MARS

Ernest Fitzgerald Anderson was a reader. Let that be known from the start. He began reading at the age of four and by the first grade was reading three grade levels ahead of his chronological age. He also possessed a productive imagination, one which proved very hard to confine with logic.

His lawyer father was not enthusiastic about the Romantic ideas of adventure and fantasy that Ernest incubated in his brain, but his mother could find no fault in his inventive and fecund mind.

His school grades reflected his intelligence; that was why his parents could not understand why he received a failing grade on a report he turned in for his science class.

Ernest was an omnivorous reader: novels, short stories, magazine and journal articles, poetry, newspapers, he enjoyed them all. Now the Menninger School had a library for each department: Primary, Intermediate, Grammar, and High School, with reading material appropriate for each level of student. The school budget didn't allow for the purchase of very many books per year, but some of the women in town made certain that there were plenty of books and magazines available through private donations. Eventually, the ladies formed the Athena Club and engendered the city library, which became their pet project.

Because of his reading prowess, Ernest was allowed to check out books from any of the four school libraries, and that is how he found the French writer Jules Verne.

Twenty Thousand Leagues Under the Sea was the first of the Verne novels that he read. He was captivated by Captain Nemo and his submarine the *Nautilus* as they prowled the oceans, seeking revenge on those governments that had hurt Nemo and his family. It wasn't so much the story of vengeance that interested Ernest, but the places that the *Nautilus* visited—Spain, the Red Sea, the islands of the South Pacific, Japan, even Atlantis—and the fight with the giant squids. All Romantic images, to be sure, but truly inspirational to Ernest.

He next tackled *Journey to the Center of the Earth*, which he found didn't measure up to the Nemo book. He was excited by the journey itself taken by Professor Otto Lidenbrock, his nephew Axel, and their guide Hans Bjelke as they descended into the bowels of the earth via a volcanic vent. He was delighted by the prehistoric animals, including mastodons, huge insects, and a large human skull that might have belonged to an ape-man that the explorers came across before being expelled through the cone of a volcano on the island of Stromboli near Italy. What left him cold were the descriptions of scientific theories and facts that Verne put in the mouth of the Professor: matters-of-fact left no room for imaginings.

The next Verne novels—*From the Earth to the Moon* and *Around the Moon*—sent him off to another author. In the former book, set just after the American Civil War, three men—the president of the Baltimore Gun Club Impy Barbicane, his enemy Captain Nicoll, and a Frenchman Michel Ardan—agreed to fly together in a projectile fired from a huge cannon to the moon. Verne discussed the size of the hole for the construction of the cannon, gravity, temperature, and other scientific features. The latter novel described the flight and the adventures the men had aboard their space "bullet," including a close encounter with an asteroid, disposing of the dead body of a dog in space, and overcoming noxious gasses. Again Verne's writing stressed the science of the experimental trip—speeds, distances, the impossibility of lunar life—things which left Ernest cold. What did ignite a fire within him were the description of the great moon crater Tycho and his wish that life existed in its mysterious depths.

Life in space became Ernest's white-hot obsession, and he turned to H.G. Wells to provide some fuel, which he found in *The First Men in the Moon*. Wells depicted a trip to the moon made by Mr. Bedford, a businessman, and Mr. Cavor, a scientist, using a steel space craft controlled by cavorite, a new material perfected by Cavor to overcome the effects of gravity. To the delight of Ernest, the two space travelers discovered a civilization of five-foot-high insect-like beings called Selenites and huge beasts called mooncalves which the Selenites used as cattle. The Selenites captured the two earthlings and took them underground, but Bedford escaped and eventually made it back to Earth. Cavor was injured and was recaptured by the Selenites, to remain on the moon with no contact with the Earth, except for some brief radio messages he sent out, but which suddenly ceased.

Ernest now had his fixation and probably would have continued in the realm of fiction except for a chance encounter he had with a donated journal. As he leafed through the pages, he came across the name Percival Lowell. It meant nothing to him, and when he read that Lowell was an astronomer, he was ready to move on until he saw the word "Mars." He decided to read the article.

Actually, it was an attack on Lowell, the founder of the Lowell Observatory in Flagstaff, Arizona, who used his twenty-four inch Clark telescope there to observe Mars and markings on the Martian surface which he thought were canals. He also saw dark spots which he thought served as oases where the canals intersected. Lowell theorized that the waterways were the final gasps of a dying Martian civilization as it tried to maintain its existence on a planet that was drying up.

Life on Mars! Ernest needed to know more. He had his mother, who was always much more sympathetic to her son's needs than his stern-faced father, order *Mars and Its Canals* and *Mars As the Abode of Life*, two of Lowell's books, even though his further reading showed him that the scientific world scoffed at Lowell's conclusions about Martian life: it was too cold for life to exist, water in a free form could not exist on the Martian surface, the "canals" and "oases" were optical illusions caused by the atmosphere.

These objections bothered Ernest not in the least: his imagination told him there was life on the Red Planet, so there must be.

He discovered an Italian named Schiaparelli linked to Lowell, so he found articles on the Italian that said by using a telescope Schiaparelli had noted not only canals on Mars, but also seas and continents which he drew on a map. Ernest could not find a copy of the Martian map, but he had no doubt that it was accurate.

When the librarian found out about his interest, she steered him to another Well's book, *The War of the Worlds*. It was set in England, but that didn't bother Ernest. Martians, who had tentacles, an oily brown skin, and were about the size of a bear, invaded the Earth after blasting off from their planet in cylinders and defeated humans by use of armored tri-pods which had heat-rays and from which poisonous black smoke could be emitted. The effect was intended by Wells to horrify readers, but Ernest was enthralled. While Wells wanted his novel to reflect the fear the English had of an invasion of their island and the fear of many religious people about the coming turn of the century (the book was published in 1898) which might usher in the end-times, for Ernest it just made him believe all the stronger that Martians were real. He fervently hoped he could meet one before their dying planet killed them all off.

Another author, Edgar Rice Burroughs, also infused young Ernest's mind with images of Martians.

In *A Princess of Mars*, John Carter, a young prospector in Arizona, hid from the Apaches in a sacred cave and awakened to find himself inexplicably transported to Mars, once a lush tropical paradise, but then a desert supplied with water only by canals. His strength was superhuman because of the lower gravity. He discovered two races of Martians: green ones with six limbs who were warlike and red ones who were human-like in form. Carter eventually sided with the red Martians, married one of their princesses, and lived happily for nine years until the Martian atmosphere began to thin after the machine that had sustained it broke down. In an attempt to save the life of his wife and the other Martians, Carter entered the factory, but was overcome and, strangely, ended up back on Earth, not knowing if he had saved the Martians or not.

In *The Gods of Mars*, Carter returned to Mars, but found himself in Valley Dor, an area from which no one was allowed to leave. He discovered the Plant Men, humanoid monsters with one eye, a tail, and a mouth in the palm of each hand by which they sucked the blood of their victims, and the Therns, white-skinned gods who enslaved or ate travelers to the Valley. A third group, the Black Pirates, also called the "First Born," were black-skinned and captured and imprisoned Carter with other slaves. He led a slave revolt, but it failed. Then there were wars, imprisonments, mutinies, cannibalism, and deaths involving different Martian groups—the Green Warriors of Warhoon, the Zodangans—out of which Carter was united with his son. His son disappeared, and Carter's wife was locked in a temple which could be unlocked only once a year. This set up a third novel, but before Ernest read it, he was given an assignment by his science teacher.

His topic was Mars.

The science teacher had heard all about Ernest's belief in life on Mars, but he was a scientist and determined that myth, legend, fantasy, and all such pipe-dreams were whimsical daydreams and sometimes even dangerous illusions. Ernest's topic was chosen by him because research in the scientific periodicals, books, and encyclopedias would convince Ernest that his belief in Martian life was based on fabrications of fanciful minds.

Ernest poured over the material. At night he peered into the heavens and gazed at the moon and the dark areas which could be the abode of beings never dreamed of by scientists. He looked at Mars, slightly red in the blackness, and imagined the straight-line canals bringing life-sustaining water from the poles to the thirsting populace of beings too readily dispatched by scientific opinion.

He stared at the scientific words—the nouns with few modifiers; the measurements of length, width, breadth, weight; the temperature scale; the matter-of-fact statements without blood, without spirit, without life.

He missed the adjectives that brought color, texture, beauty, courage, horror, life itself to the written page and to the mind and feelings of the reader of that page.

Ernest began typing.

When his parents came to the meeting they had requested with the science teacher, he was only too glad to show them Ernest's report and the red "F" he had scribbled at the top of the first page.

After looking at the report, Ernest's father handed it to his wife, convinced they had no case for a grade reversal.

Ernest's mother took her time and read every word. She felt that Ernest should at least get a passing grade for Creativity.

The paper began, "As the flying bullet-like craft descended through the reddish Martian atmosphere, suddenly the water-filled canals appeared. Reflecting the atmosphere, the water looked red to Captain Bartholomew Magellan of the United States Army. He eased down over the narrow strip of water surrounded by patches of some kind of vegetation. Suddenly he saw movement beside a tree-like growth. There it was again. A great head peered around the tree and opened its mouth in a tremendous roar which Magellan could not hear inside his cylinder. It didn't matter; all he could think was 'There is life on Mars.'"

MAGGIE FACES LIFE

— 🌀 —

Maggie Vogler could hardly wait for school to begin. She would be in the ninth grade, a freshman. No one in her family had ever gotten that far before. Her mother Hedy had to quit after the eighth grade, and her father, or the man called her father, never made it past the sixth grade.

Manfred Friedrich Vogler was an alcoholic who had become so abusive to Maggie that Hedy finally left him when the family lived in Fargo. M.F., as Maggie called him, had spent time in the Cass County jail, and he was still a prisoner when the divorce was finalized. Upon his release he had headed for the West Coast. The support payments Hedy was supposed to receive never found their way to Menninger, North Dakota, where Hedy, Maggie, and her brother and sister, seven-year old Johnny and four-year old Alys, lived.

Hedy had been so proud back in May when Maggie received her eighth-grade diploma in a ceremony at the Park School. Maggie wore the cotton dress her mother had made special for the occasion, and Miss Fenton, Maggie's favorite teacher, had complimented the dress and congratulated Maggie on her educational achievements. It had been a great day.

The summer had gone by so quickly. Her mother ran Hedy's Haven, a restaurant on Villard Avenue, and was busy all the time, trying to make a go of it in hard times. Later, the Stock Market Crash of 1929 seemed to many Americans as the start of the Great Depression, but in the farming states a depressed economy had begun several years earlier. Small towns like Menninger were reeling financially.

Maggie's summer job was to care for Johnny and Alys while Mama was at work. Every so often she got to see her friends, Aggie, Hilda, and Tillie. Twice that summer she'd gone with them to a movie at the Blackstone Theatre—*Kid Boots*, a comedy with Eddie Cantor and Clara Bow, and *The Black Pirate*, starring Douglas Fairbanks and Billie Dove. Maggie liked the movies, but felt a little uneasy because her friends had bought her ticket, and she never had enough money to pay their way.

Johnny and Alys were asleep after a hard day of play. As she waited for her mother, Maggie ran over in her mind the items she would need for school and hoped there would be a little money for an extra dress.

It seemed to be taking her mother an extra-long time to get home. She went out onto the steps. The wind stirred the reeds in the marsh just to the south, and she heard a train whistle crying out its presence far off in the distance.

She looked at the hole in the front window. Johnny had thrown his beat-up baseball, missed his target by a mile, and now the baseball lay between the storm window and the inside pane. It would have to remain there until Mama had enough money to get the glass replaced. Mama said, "No glass; no baseball." An old piece of gray cloth had been stuffed in the hole, keeping out the elements.

She walked around the corner of the house and looked up the hill. There was no one in sight. She went back inside and got a book Miss Fenton had given her on her graduation, *The Story of Dr. Dolittle* about a man who could talk to animals. At first, she thought it a little strange, but soon she was enjoying her time spent with the book.

When her mother walked in, Maggie could see something was wrong. After learning the other two children were asleep, Mama sat with Maggie, her head down.

"What's wrong, Mama?"

There was a reluctance at first, but finally her mother owned up to what she had to say. "I've lost the restaurant." Her head sagged and she stared at the table.

"Don't worry, Mama. We can make other money." Maggie didn't know how, but she had to say something.

Hedy looked at Maggie. "I guess there are just too many restaurants in town, what with the people who've left and the farmers cutting back. I've been to the county and we can get on relief, but it won't be enough; we could lose the house, too."

"I won't let that happen; I'll get a job after school."

Hedy took Maggie's hands in hers. "Maggie, I'm…afraid there won't be any school for you this year."

Maggie was paralyzed: she couldn't speak; she could hardly think.

"I can't pack up and leave town again; it's not fair to Johnny and Alys. But you hold the key, Maggie, if you'll do it."

The words were filtering in, but Maggie had no idea what her mother was talking about. How could she have the key?

"I talked with a man; his brother owns a restaurant in Breckenridge, Michalski's. He's always looking for help. If you…would give up school for a couple years…work in Breckenridge, send some money home, the kids and I would be all right. It'll be tight, but…."

Maggie's world melted like sugar castles in the rain. She got up and put her arms around her mother's shoulders. "I'll do it, Mama…it's time I grew up."

Two days later Hedy, Johnny, and Alys walked Maggie the block to the station. Maggie hadn't told her friends she wouldn't be in school anymore. What good would that do? Just cause a bunch of tears and what good would they do?

There were tears when Maggie said goodbye and hugged her family; there were more tears, quiet ones reflecting in the window of the coach, as the locomotive puffed out black smoke and pulled the train into motion.

Maggie took out the note her mother had given her. Michalski was supposed to have taken care of everything, so she would be expected, and a room in a cheap rooming house would be ready. There were directions to the rooming house and to Michalski's Restaurant.

As the train rolled on, Maggie got to feeling pretty blue. Most of the other passengers, mostly men, were quiet. Two small children, a boy and a girl, were with a young woman, probably their mother. She was having a difficult time: they wanted to run up and down the aisles, and she was clutching them to her body so only their blonde heads showed and was trying to explain why they couldn't.

Maggie decided the kids were the young woman's problem and tried to rest, but the crying and occasional screaming wouldn't let her. Finally, she decided to help. The kids were about the same ages as her brother and sister, so she should be able to handle them.

It turned out she only had to handle the boy. The little girl turned shy and decided to stay with her mother. The little boy, Charlie, went with Maggie and she told him stories—fairy tales, book stories she had read, ones she made up—until they stopped at Fargo and the family got off. The mother couldn't thank Maggie enough and Charlie gave her a hug. She did have a way with children.

As she watched the little family leave the platform, she noticed the depot itself. The building didn't appear much bigger than the depot in Menninger, but it was brown brick and not wood painted white. She liked the large clock tower that stuck up from the middle of the building and held the face of a clock on the sides she could see.

The whistle and bell sounded, and the train began to move between the back-ends and sides of Fargo's buildings. They went into a curve; the buildings stayed on the left, but the right side fell away toward the Red River. They headed into Moorhead, clattering across a bridge over the placid and dirty water.

It didn't make any sense, but ever since the depot, Maggie had been scrunched down in the seat just in case M.F. had returned and was looking into the train from who knew where—the embankment, an alley, a blind pig?

The tracks curved into Fargo's little Minnesota neighbor and then straightened to the east. Another curve and the train passed between buildings with the dreary sameness of old wood, faded paint, and piles of refuse, hidden from the streets, but plainly visible from the passing trains.

Clearing the Moorhead yards, the locomotive steamed south, dragging its string of complaining cars along. The land was flat and covered in crops—grains and something Maggie thought might be potatoes. Occasionally a small line of trees would rush by in the ditch, but it was rare to see farm buildings along the tracks.

The steady clack of the wheels and the swaying of the coach were so steady that Maggie's eyes began to close. The sound of the whistle just before a crossing and the extended whistle and the slowing down as the train passed through a town or village kept her from a deep sleep. Comstock, Wolverton, Kent, Brushvale, all passed like images in a dream forgotten in the morning.

The noise of a bridge-crossing roused Maggie from her unfinished rest, but she closed her eyes again and actual sleep came. It didn't last long: the conductor awakened her with the call of "Brixton!" A bustle of departing and boarding passengers and then another bridge across the Red River and another call: "Breckenridge!"

After she had collected her two travel bags, Maggie crossed a sidetrack and began walking down Minnesota Avenue, looking for Michalski's. At first there were false-front wooden buildings, none too prosperous; Maggie didn't like what she saw. Then she noticed brick buildings coming up; she hoped the restaurant was in one of them. It was.

During the bad years railroad men who were lucky enough to keep their jobs had more money than the average citizen, so businesses that catered to the "rails" did well. Michalski's was down the street from the GN depot; Breckenridge was a railroad division point with a round house and shops; Michalski's did well.

When Maggie saw the sign and the clean windows, she felt certain that it was a good place to eat and work and not a hash house, which her mother called eating places that were not worth going into and whose owners didn't care if you did or not.

She asked the woman behind the counter where she could find Mr. Michalski. "In the kitchen, back there." She pointed. "If yuh want, yuh can leave those behind here." She pointed at the bags and then where she was standing.

Maggie wasn't too sure about leaving them, but it wouldn't be a good start not to trust her fellow workers, so she put her bags by the woman. "Thank you." The woman went to the till where a customer waited.

Paulie Michalski stood about five-feet four on a hot day; on cold days he seemed shorter. He wore a black bowler hat, a black suit (he had taken off his coat: it was on a hanger which was on a hook), white shirt with black sleeve garters, and a huge handlebar mustache, also black. When he worked in the kitchen, he wore a white apron that dropped almost to his ankles.

Just as Maggie walked through the swinging doors, he was cursing and shouting his displeasure at something a waitress was about to serve. Maggie was frightened. After the waitress went to get a different plate, Michalski looked at Maggie. "Well?"

"I…I'm your new waitress, sir." The words could barely be heard above the kitchen noise. Michalski motioned her to follow him. In his office she explained how she'd been hired.

He looked her over. "How old are you?"

"Eighteen."

"You don't look over fourteen."

"I just turned eighteen. I've always looked younger."

"Fine. I suppose you've had experience since your mother runs a restaurant."

"Yes." Maggie felt awkward with her lies, but Mama said it would be all right; Maggie could ask the Lord's forgiveness after she started work.

"You have to wear a uniform, fresh every day; all my waitresses do. You can leave 'em here and we'll send 'em to a laundry with the charge deducted from your pay, or you can take two, wash 'em in your sink, and save some money; your landlady has an iron and a board. Can you wash clothes and iron 'em?"

Maggie couldn't count the times she had done her family's clothes. "Yes, sir."

"Do you have a sturdy pair of shoes? You'll need 'em. Nothin' worse than bad shoes for a waitress."

Her mother had sent along a good pair of shoes in one of the bags. "Yes, sir."

"All right, then. Come in tomorrow at eleven. We'll start you out easy. You'll be stayin' on Nebraska Avenue. Know where that is?"

"No, sir."

"Walk down to the corner, turn left; it's the next street. Your rooming house is to the right a couple blocks." He got up. "I don't pay as much as you'd get in a department store, but the tips will make up for it. Especially if the rails like you. Make sure you smile at the customers. Pick up your uniforms on the way out."

"Thank you, sir." He was already gone.

Her landlady was Michalski's sister Amy; she was taller than her brother (who wasn't?), cheerful in contrast to his gruff, and had graying hair. Her husband Samuel Alford was the handyman around the rooming house.

The room was small and neat with a window for the sunlight, and it even opened for fresh air, but the walls were a dark gloomy brown. The room was furnished with the requisite furniture items and a bed that had a solid mattress. Maggie could eat discounted meals in Michalski's kitchen, but there was a hot plate in the room for warming up soup, stew, or other canned goods.

Maggie liked the room, except for the color, and thought Mrs. Alford was nice. She wasn't certain about Michalski, especially his yelling, but things should work out when he saw what a hard worker she was.

She hadn't eaten since breakfast, so she went to a little grocery and bought a small loaf of bread and a jar of peanut butter. She made a sandwich for supper, washed it down with water, got ready for bed after brushing her teeth with the toothbrush and tooth powder her mother had packed, and crawled under the covers.

She said her prayers, including a request for forgiveness for lying and safety for herself and her family. The sounds in the rooming house and the excitement of starting her job kept her awake for a long time.

The next morning she was up early and ate peanut butter and bread for breakfast. When she put on her uniform, she saw that Fern, the counter woman, had sized her almost perfectly. She went down to the main floor and watched the clock approach eleven, then walked out the door, with Mrs. Alford's "Good luck" sending her on her way.

Michalski's was a mad house. A passenger train had been delayed by a broken rail down the line, so many of the travelers had gotten off to stretch their legs and grab a meal. Train food was pricey.

Fern shoved an order pad, pencil, and four menus into Maggie's hands and told her to wait on tables. "Take number 3." She pointed. "Just yell the order in at the window; the cooks will know. And smile."

Maggie didn't have time to be nervous. She approached the table with a smile and handed out the menus. "Would you like some water?" That's what the waitresses in Hedy's Haven said.

The men smiled back. "Yes, and coffee all around," a man with black hair said and made a circling gesture.

Maggie hustled to the line of percolaters behind the counter, poured four cups, and looked at Fern, who pointed to a stack of trays. Maggie placed the steaming cups on the top one and headed for the table. She thought waitressing wasn't so bad.

When the black-haired man said he wanted a #1, Maggie had to look at the menu under Specials. There it was: #1—hot beef sandwich with mashed potatoes and beef gravy, cut green beans, dinner roll and butter, slice of apple or cherry pie, coffee.

She wrote down every item and turned to the next man, who wanted the same. As she wrote, it seemed the men were exchanging looks. She wrote down the list of items for a #3 Special, but the last man just wanted a sandwich, so Maggie wrote "one hamburger sandwich, well done, with lettuce and tomato, no mayonnaise (she hoped she had spelled that correctly) or onions."

She dropped the menus in their box on the way to the kitchen window. Another waitress was just walking away; she smiled and Maggie smiled back. She held up her pad and shouted, "One hot beef sandwich with mashed potatoes and beef gravy, cut green beans, dinner roll and butter, slice of apple pie." She left off the coffee because the man already had his cup. Just as she started on her second order, she glanced at Mr. Michalski. He was standing with his bowler pushed far back on his head, his hands on his hips, and his mouth an open circle, dark eyes riveted on her.

"What in the hell did Arnie send us now!"

Maggie didn't know what to do, so she kept on with the second order until Michalski asked for the pad and ordered her into the kitchen. He looked over the orders, began filling them, and yelled across to the man at the large sink, "Jack, here's another bubble dancer." Jack motioned a bewildered Maggie over to him.

"Here." He handed her a large towel. "Dry those plates and stack 'em over there." She did as she was told and continued to follow Jack's orders until well after the rush was over. When things returned to normal, Michalski said to her, "Come with me."

Seated across from him in his office, Maggie began to cry. Michalski sat there for a minute or so, but she didn't stop. He got up and walked out. When he returned, he put a chocolate milk shake in front of her. "Go ahead." It was one of the best things she'd ever tasted, and when she saw him smiling at her, it was even better.

"You've never been a waitress, have you?" The words brought forth more tears; he waited until she was done. "Well?"

"No."

"Why did you lie?"

Maggie explained. When she finished, he said, "All right, we'll make a waitress out of you yet." He told her how to call just the numbers of the Specials to the cooks; they knew what went into each special. If a customer didn't want something that was part of a Special or a combination, she should say, "86 onions" or "86 veg." Well-done would be "kill it" or "burn it." He talked for five minutes, then realized she'd never remember everything he'd said, so he repeated the first two and told her she'd pick up the rest.

He also made her promise never to lie to him again.

She hadn't had time for dinner, so she stopped by the grocery. For supper she had brown beans warmed on the hot plate, bread which she used to soak up the juice, and water. She went to bed early with a sore back.

The next day she did better, and the tips jingled in her pocket on the way to the store, where she bought some canned corn, Vienna sausages, and a box of Lux Soap Flakes. That night she washed her uniform and borrowed Mrs. Alford's electric iron and board, which became a nightly routine.

As she grew more accustomed to the ways of the restaurant, Maggie wasn't so intimidated by Michalski. She learned more about good waitressing, and she made some friends. Fern was older, but all the girls were. More her age, but still four or five years older, were Kitty from Parkers Prairie, a town even smaller than Menninger, and Josepha, who wanted to be called Josie, from a farm southeast of Breckenridge near Campbell.

The waitresses worked a six-day week, followed by a five-day week, and then back into the six/five rotation. Most of the time on her days off, Maggie would rest in her room, read some of Mrs. Alford's magazines or books, or go for walks. Walks didn't cost anything. Neither did reading. She read in the *Bible*, tried an old battered copy of *The Pilgrim's Progress*, but put it down as too difficult, and enjoyed looking through the pages of *McCall's Magazine*, *Ladies' Home Journal*, and *Woman's Home Companion*. She found *The Wizard of Oz*, a book she had started when her family was living in Aberdeen, South Dakota, but never got to finish. After a couple of evenings, she did finish it and felt good that Dorothy had made it home. She found herself wishing for a companion like Toto, so she wouldn't be so lonely.

She also remembered how in Aberdeen she would have liked a pair of silver shoes like Dorothy's, then she looked at her own brown ones and had to smile.

Sometimes on her walks, she'd look at the people or study the buildings. She heard there were over two thousand people in Breckenridge, and with what she saw, she could believe it. Some of the buildings were especially interesting: the three-story brick Hotel Stratford with a Land & Loan company on the first floor; the Catholic Church with a large main steeple and two smaller steeples on each side of it; the Wilkin County Courthouse that looked somewhat like a church with its steeple, except it had a flag pole, not a cross, on top. The high school was also fronted by a tower that was steeple-like. The brick St. Francis Hospital looked like three separate buildings linked into one. The middle structure had a little tower sticking out of the roof, and there were smaller ones on the other two. Breckenridge certainly liked its steeples and towers. The bustle of Minnesota Avenue between Fourth and Sixth streets made her feel like she was serving a truly living community when she waited on some of the people at Michalski's. She liked to be of service.

She also liked to stroll around the large Benesh & Pierce Department Store, but did not buy anything, except a chemise to wear in her room.

In the middle of Minnesota Avenue, she saw street car tracks. They ran west from the Great Northern depot to Brixton. She would have liked to have ridden in one of the cars, but Michalski told her the company had folded the year before. The car house had been over on 6th Street.

If her days off got too long and she wasn't too tired, she'd watch the activity in the Great Northern yards just across Minnesota. There were almost always trains pulling in or out, switch engines moving cars around, metallic and mechanical noises coming from the roundhouse and the shops.

One day when both Josie and she had their two consecutive days-off together, Josie's parents came up in a rickety Ford Model T, and the four of them squeezed together for the fifteen-mile return trip to Campbell. After supper they all went to a barn dance.

Maggie expected an old dirty barn like the one that was decaying behind the Oleson House in Menninger, so she was delighted by the clean wooden floor and the bright lights. She had never been to a dance, but Josie and her friends showed her the intricacies of square dancing, and a tall Swedish boy named Per was happy to help her learn the two-step and waltz. Walking her to the Model T, he said he'd stop in and see her whenever he was in Breckenridge. She thought that would be nice.

The next morning she went to church with the family, who sat in their own pew. Part of the sermon was devoted to caring for the sick, the poor, the outcasts; the minister used the lepers and their disgusting flesh as an example. After dinner (Josie and she insisted on doing the dishes), they all drove back to Breckenridge. It was the best day Maggie had yet experienced. She and Josie became even better friends, but then Josie quit her job and left for a new one in Fargo. Per never did stop by to see Maggie and his face faded from her memory.

Maggie felt very proud of herself when she opened a checking account at the Farmers & Merchants State Bank. After that she would send a check home to her mother, along with a letter, every two weeks. Even better, she'd get a response every time, telling her the news of the family, her friends, and the town. Her mother was so grateful for the money; it was enough to keep the family afloat. Whatever her mother spent the money on, she would tell Maggie about it: new pants for Johnny, new shoes for Alys. Johnny would always sign his name, now that he was in second grade, and Alys would make a scrawl. Reading and re-reading the letters made Maggie happy and sad at the same time.

Seeing the school girls come into Michalski's and order ice cream or sodas at the counter and talk about what was going on in school made Maggie sad.

As autumn's winds tore down summer's leaves, Maggie noticed her body was aching more than it had. She thought the longer she worked, the stronger her body would become, but her back and feet were in pain. She borrowed a pail from Samuel and would soak her sore feet every night in warm water and Epsom salts.

Something else that caused her pain was the "curse." It first came on her while she was still at home, and her mother was there to sooth her fears that she was dying.

The onset of the "curse" brought severe cramps. Some days she didn't even think she could go to work, but knowing how her family depended on her, she pushed her way through the day and collapsed on her bed almost as soon as she got home.

When she was suffering, she was embarrassed to go to the women's rest room so many times to change her pad because she was certain everyone, even the men, knew why.

Just as embarrassing was going to the drug store to buy the blue box of Kotex. Even though the male clerk seemed to ring up her purchase and bag it in a matter-of-fact way, she was sure he was snickering inside. She wished a woman would take his place.

By November the cloth coat she had brought wasn't enough to keep her warm, especially her bare legs, as she walked to work, so she bought a long winter coat at Benesh & Pierce, and, thinking ahead, a pair of boots, also. She apologized in her next letter for the small amount she sent home with it, but her mother's letter was very understanding.

Thanksgiving was a godsend. Michalski's was a twenty-four hour restaurant, except for Sundays and certain holidays. Thanksgiving was one of them. After he locked the door, Michalski set out a dinner of turkey and all the trimmings for any of his employees that didn't have a home to go to. A dishwasher, a cook, and five waitresses were his guests. Maggie enjoyed listening to the conversation of the others almost as much as the food.

The next day it was back to work, and the routine kept up until Christmas when Michalski took care of his employees again.

On New Year's Eve the restaurant closed just after midnight, but there was no food for the employees. The next day the cook and the dishwasher showed up with hangovers. Maggie just showed up.

It had been a frigid walk to work and it took her awhile to get her circulation going. While she was waiting on table 5, the door opened and a rather large woman walked in. She opened her green coat to reveal a shiny purple, red, and gold dress. She wore a large hat with pheasant feathers and a couple fake flowers and sported black high-heeled boots. Kitty waited on her and the two men, younger and conservatively dressed, who were with her. Kitty didn't seem to want to do the waiting, but it was her table.

When Kitty went back with the order, Michalski poked his head out of the kitchen, a scowl darkening his face.

After the lady and her friends finished, she caught Maggie by the arm and said, "I haven't seen you here before. Are you new?"

"No, I started last August."

"My, my. Do you like it?"

"Yes, I do."

"Well, that's good. I run a restaurant, too, and I like it when my employees like to work for me. Maybe we'll talk again."

After she finished her shift, Michalski took her into his office. "I saw you talkin' with Big Min."

"Is that her name?"

"Minnie Rader. Stay away from her; she's no good. Don't ever work for her; it's trouble."

"What kind of trouble?"

Michalski reddened. "Just take my word for it. It's no place for young girls. Promise me you won't ever work for Big Min."

"I promise." Maggie wondered about the conversation all the way home and then forgot about it. Her work shoes were too small and her feet were killing her.

She was walking home a month later when she realized it was her birthday. She stopped at the bakery and bought a chocolate cupcake. She borrowed a little candle from Mrs. Alford and put in on the cupcake which she had for dessert. The candle and the birthday card which her mother had sent reminded her of the birthdays she'd had at home and for the first time in months she cried herself to sleep.

A month later Mrs. Alford had to go to the St. Francis with pneumonia. Her life was despaired of at one point, but she started to recover. Michalski spent a lot of time with her.

One day while he was at the hospital, Big Min and her two men appeared. Big Min in a bright yellow dress and hat trimmed with purple-dyed ostrich feathers asked specially for Maggie as her waitress. After the three finished their food, they waited until Maggie took her break, then asked her to join them.

The reason was Big Min wanted Maggie to work for her. She knew what Michalski paid Maggie and offered to double her wages, if she'd do a little work on the side. When Maggie asked her what, Big Min was evasive, but said it wouldn't interfere with her waitressing job. "I'll be back in a week, so make up your mind by then. There are other girls who'll jump at the chance."

Maggie didn't know what she should do; Michalski had been so good to her, but he could also be gruff when things didn't go right and had refused to give her a raise the two times she'd asked. When she went to Fern and Kitty about Big Min, they clammed up, but indicated she should have nothing to do with her.

The crusher came when she finally went to Benesh & Pierce for new shoes. She couldn't believe how much they cost. Her family needed the money, but she did need the shoes. Her feet were swollen so much she could barely get into her old ones.

A week later wearing gaudy forest green and gold, Big Min and her plainly dressed bodyguards came in and once again asked for Maggie. When Big Min brought up the job offer, Maggie said she would go to work at her restaurant, only she didn't know where it was. Big Min gave her directions and said Maggie'd be staying on the second floor of the building. Maggie thought how nice that would be, not having to walk through snow drifts to work. The restaurant was south of the tracks near some old warehouses. Maggie had never been to that neighborhood before.

When she finished the next day, Maggie asked to speak to Michalski in his office. She couldn't look him in the eye when she said she had a different job and was giving him notice.

He stared at her for a long time, then burst out with curses and ended up with "You little piss ant! Here I train you to be the best waitress in the place and this is the thanks I get!"

"I…I'm sorry. I…."

"Tell me one thing; you're not goin' over to Big Min's?"

"No, I'm not," she lied.

"'cus if you do, anything you get there will be too good for you."

"I'm not. But I'm sorry…truly…."

"Get out! Get out now! Have Fern give you the money you earned and don't ever come back, you ungrateful whelp!" He stormed back to the kitchen.

It took Maggie quite awhile to stop crying and fix her face enough to talk to Fern.

Mrs. Alford was very sorry to see her go, but said she could have a room there any time.

Big Min took Maggie under her wing and put her to work almost immediately. Maggie noticed that the clientele was a lot different than that of Michalski's. Ninety percent men and most of them tough working men from the train crews, the shops and roundhouse, and others that sounded to her like bootleggers, blind pigs, and others that knew their way around the Volstead Act. There were also some business types that looked very ill at ease and overly loud college boys from across the river in Brixton.

She didn't care for the other waitresses. They all seemed to have a hard edge, used some pretty bad language, and didn't want her friendship. She longed to see Kitty's freckles and to hear Fern's soft voice.

The girls all had rooms on the second floor, staggered on either side of a long dark hallway. Her room certainly wasn't any worse than the one she'd had at the rooming house. Maggie was grateful Big Min put her way down on the end with no neighbors, but she thought it strange that sometimes she could hear men's voices in the hall at night.

When she asked Big Min why there were no locks on the doors, she laughed and said, "Don't worry about that. Al and Johnny take better care of you girls than any lock ever could."

Maggie made out very well; the tips were bigger than at Michalski's and with what Big Min was going to pay her, she'd be able to send a lot more home. Of course, she had to put up with the lustful stares of some of the men and the occasional pat on her bottom, but Big Min would step in and tell the offender to back off or get out. Maggie appreciated that.

After two weeks she got her pay—more than Michalski would pay her in a month. Big Min was a savior. When Big Min handed her the money, she asked if Maggie was ready for her side work. If she was any good, it would pay extra. Maggie couldn't believe she'd get even more money and said she was ready. She waited for Big Min to take her to the kitchen to learn to be a cook, but the woman just smiled and walked away.

Even Big Min couldn't help Maggie's feet. Despite her new shoes, her feet ached, her toes throbbed, and there were small corns beginning to grow.

The next evening after supper, Maggie was sitting on the bed in her underwear and chemise. Her bra lay over a chair and her feet were soaking in a pail. Suddenly the door opened and a man stepped into the room. "Are you the new girl?" He had on the uniform of a railroad conductor.

Maggie had grabbed the towel and clutched it against her breasts. "Who are you? What do you want?"

"What? You know what I want. I already paid Big Min."

He stepped closer and Maggie shrank back against the headboard. "Honest, mister, I don't know what you want."

He looked closely at her. "How old are you?"

She didn't answer.

"Do you know what this place is?"

"Yes, it's a restaurant. I work downstairs. You shouldn't be here."

He sat in the chair and was quiet. He looked at her with softening eyes. Maggie toweled her feet and got under the covers. "You have to go or I'll call Big Min."

"I don't think that would help." The man sat there, looking around at the bare walls of the room, then staring not so much at her as at the bed. He started to speak a couple of times; it was like he knew what he wanted to say, but his mind was all mixed up.

Then it came out. "I just realized what a stinkin' rat I've been comin' here tonight. I have a wonderful wife in Willmar and a daughter about your age, and I almost threw them away out of a moment of weakness."

He went on to tell her she had to get away from that place and why.

Maggie didn't know very much about sex and what little she knew came from her girlfriends. She thought what they told her was mostly lies, and when Tillie described what married people did in bed, Maggie thought such an act was the most disgusting thing she'd ever heard of and never let Tillie speak about it again.

Maggie was going to talk to her mother about it, but she never overcame the embarrassment which would have tagged along with the asking.

As a result Maggie was totally unprepared when the railroad man told her what men paid for at Big Min's besides food. When he finished, she wanted to leave so badly her skin felt like what the lepers in the *Bible* must have felt. She hadn't wanted to believe Tillie, but she had been right. The conductor said he would help her and went into the hallway while she got dressed.

As they walked downstairs, there were some catcalls from the man's friends until they saw his face. Big Min, not quite as colorful in a black and white dress and a black turban with a white tassel and trimmed with pearls, came up to them. "Where d'ya think you're goin'?"

The conductor said, "She's goin' away from here."

"Oh, no, she's not." Big Min put her fingers to her mouth and out came a loud whistle. Her two bodyguards materialized from a side room.

The conductor dropped the two bags, pushed Maggie behind him, and squared off.

All the rails in the place jumped to their feet. Some of the other customers fled the scene, but many of them stood with Big Min, who was yelling at Maggie to get back upstairs. Maggie's knees weakened and she almost sat down.

Two rails jumped up beside the conductor and faced off with the bodyguards. Tables and chairs were scraped aside in anticipation of a coming brawl. Men were yelling, but Big Min's voice could be heard above everything else, threatening Maggie to get to her room and damning the conductor to everlasting Hell.

Suddenly the conductor raised his arms and held up his hands, palms out. "Boys! Boys!" The room began to quiet. "Boys, we can't let anything happen to this little girl!" The noise started again, sprinkled with jeers. "Boys, you can't! It's not right!" More jeering and a loud horselaugh from Big Min. "You can't...we can't...she's still...fresh!"

Maggie wasn't certain what that meant, but she burst into tears. The air went out of the room, and it grew so peaceful that just Maggie's sobs and a faraway train whistle could be heard.

Then Big Min made a grab for Maggie and the bodyguards moved with her. Immediately they were struck down, not just by the rails, but by some of Big Min's regular customers. Maggie was hustled out and a crowd of men walked with her, carrying her bags and guarding her.

They crossed the tracks to Minnesota Avenue, where the conductor thanked them all. Most of them left for their homes, too ashamed to say anything to Maggie. The conductor's train crew walked Maggie to the Alford Rooming House, which was the only place she could think of to go.

Mrs. Alford was so glad to see her, she had a room immediately. Maggie thanked the train crew and especially the conductor, but like the other men his embarrassment made him leave with hardly a word.

The next morning Maggie asked Mrs. Alford if she thought her brother would hire her back.

"Oh, no, my dear. Paulie is terribly upset and angry with you. He says you lied to him. He knows about you going over to Big Min, and after you told him you weren't. He can't trust you and he won't have an employee he can't trust. He was hoping you would be head waitress someday, but all that's gone now. Oh, no, Paulie'd never take you back."

Maggie needed a job and finally found one at Jack's, a lunch counter and pie and ice cream place toward the river. Jack wore a beret to cover his baldness and always had a toothpick in the corner of his mouth. He said he'd put her on a trial basis.

The trial became permanent once Jack realized he had hired a curiosity piece. His little three-booth, three-table, fifteen-foot counter place had never been busier than after people found out the young girl who had escaped from Big Min was working there.

High school boys came in to see if she'd go out with them ("No, but thank you anyway."). Church ladies and Lodge women came to talk to her, to ask her to speak to their groups, to come to church or join their organization, but Maggie always turned them down. Businessmen came in just to look, as if she were an exotic animal in a cage.

Maggie was getting desperate. She needed the job, but she didn't appreciate being treated like some sideshow freak. It was spring; the trees, flowers, and birds were telling her to be happy, but her world had become limited to Jack's and the rooming house. No more walks, no more barn dances, no more Kitty or Fern.

Then one day a letter, the best one ever. Her mother had found a job as a cook at the Menninger Café in the Menninger Arms Hotel. There was also a place for a waitress, so Maggie must get home as quickly as possible.

The next day she told Jack she was quitting. He was going to put up a fuss about not giving him the two weeks that was customary, but he stopped when she said he could keep what he owed her. He decided that two weeks wasn't necessary and gave her half of what she had coming. She didn't care; she thanked him.

She said her goodbyes to Mrs. Alford. Even Samuel came up from the basement for a hug.

She closed out her bank account and went to the depot. After she bought her ticket and checked her baggage, it was dinner time. She went across the tracks and walked Minnesota as she had done her first day. She went to Michalski's and asked for Kitty. It was good to talk with her again. Fern had gotten engaged and moved back home to New York Mills, so there was a new woman behind the counter, but she was pleasant.

Maggie kept looking for Michalski; she wanted to tell him how she sorry she was about not living up to what he deserved in an employee, but he never came out of the kitchen. She could hear him sometimes, thundering at some mistake someone other than he had made, but she was too fearful about what he would say to her to go back there.

She left Kitty a good tip.

Her train didn't leave until the evening, so she paced the station and the platform or waited anxiously on the bench until she heard the whistle and the clanging of the bell as the locomotive pulled in.

From her window, she watched Breckenridge pass by, then the river, then Brixton, and then the flat farmland of the Valley. The whistle, the bell, Moorhead, and a stop; the river again, then whistle-bell-Fargo and another stop; passengers in and out both places, but Maggie only wished they would hurry: home was waiting.

She had bought a couple cookies and a doughnut in Breckenridge and they made up her supper.

They also made her sleepy, and she dozed through the ten or so little towns attached to the tracks where the railroad needed grain-shipping points.

Finally, whistle-bell-Menninger. She got off and found her bags. Off the platform and up the sidewalk on Dakota Street. The marsh still there on the left with some frogs sounding off. Just beyond, her house, white in the moonlight.

As she went up the steps, she saw Johnny's baseball was no longer in the window; the broken glass had been replaced. That made Maggie feel good.

She let herself in and put down the bags. It was quiet; Johnny and Alys would be safe in their beds. There was a light on in the kitchen and there was her mother. She was seated at the table, half a glass of milk and the crumbs from a small piece of chocolate cake on a plate off to the side.

An opened *Bible* was in front of her. She was breathing softly. Maggie saw she had fallen asleep.

She had started a letter—

"My Dearest Daughter,

"I can hardly wait to see your smiling…"

Maggie kissed her on the forehead; her mother stirred and looked at her through sleep-fogged eyes.

"Maggie?"

It was good to be home.